A WHISPER
IN THE NIGHT

BOOKS BY JOAN AIKEN

Foul Matter
The Girl from Paris
The Weeping Ash
The Smile of the Stranger
Castle Barebane
The Five-Minute Marriage
Last Movement
The Silence of Herondale

Voices in an Empty House
A Cluster of Separate
    Sparks
The Embroidered Sunset
The Crystal Crow
Dark Interval
Beware of the Bouquet
The Fortune Hunters

JUVENILES

A Touch of Chill
The Shadow Guests
The Stolen Lake
The Skin Spinners: Poems
The Green Flash and
    Other Tales
The Far Forests: Tales of
    Romance, Fantasy and
    Suspense
The Angel Inn by the
    Comtesse de Segur,
    translated by Joan Aiken
Go Saddle the Sea
The Faithless Lollybird
Not What You Expected
Arabel's Raven
The Mooncusser's
    Daughter: A Play
    for Children

Arabel and Mortimer
Winterthing: A Children's
    Play
Street: A Play for Children
The Cuckoo Tree
Midnight Is a Place
Died on a Rainy Sunday
Night Fall
Smoke from Cromwell's
    Time and Other Stories
The Whispering Mountain
A Necklace of Raindrops
Armitage, Armitage Fly
    Away Home
Nightbirds on Nantucket
Black Hearts in Battersea
The Wolves of Willoughby
    Chase
Bridle the Wind

A WHISPER
IN THE NIGHT
Tales of Terror and Suspense

~~~~~~~~~~~~~~~~~~~~~~~~~~~

JOAN AIKEN

DELACORTE PRESS / NEW YORK

Published by
Delacorte Press
1 Dag Hammarskjold Plaza
New York, N.Y. 10017

A Whisper in the Night was first published, in a different form, in Great Britain by Victor Gollancz Ltd.

The following stories in this book were previously published: "Finders Weepers" in *Black Eyes and Other Spine Chillers,* Pepper Press; "The Windowbox Waltz" in *Girl's Choice: A Collection of Stories* (Copyright © The Hamlyn Publishing Group Ltd., 1965, 1979), "Two Races" in *Isaac Asimov Science Fiction Magazine,* "Old Fillikin" in *The Twilight Zone Magazine,* "Homer's Whistle" in *They Wait* edited by Lance Salway, Pepper Press.

Library of Congress Cataloging in Publication Data
Aiken, Joan, [date of birth]
A whisper in the night.
Contents: Lob's girl—Miss Spitfire—Finders keepers—[etc.]
1. Horror tales, English. [1. Horror stories.
2. Short stories] I. Title.
PZ7.A2695Wf 1984   [Fic]   84-3247
ISBN 0-385-29344-5

MANUFACTURED IN THE UNITED STATES OF AMERICA
FIRST PRINTING

To Charles Schlessiger

Contents

A WHISPER
IN THE NIGHT

Lob's Girl

~~~~~~

Some people choose their dogs, and some dogs choose their people. The Pengelly family had no say in the choosing of Lob; he came to them in the second way, and very decisively.

It began on the beach, the summer when Sandy was five, Don, her older brother, twelve, and the twins were three. Sandy was really Alexandra, because her grandmother had a beautiful picture of a queen in a diamond tiara and high collar of pearls. It hung by Granny Pearce's kitchen sink and was as familiar as the doormat. When Sandy was born everyone agreed that she was the living spit of the picture, and so she was called Alexandra and Sandy for short.

On this summer day she was lying peacefully reading a comic and not keeping an eye on the twins, who didn't need it because they were occupied in seeing which of them could wrap the most seaweed around the other one's legs. Father—Bert Pengelly—and Don were up on the Hard painting the bottom boards of the boat in which Father went fishing for pilchards. And Mother—Jean Pengelly—was getting ahead with making the Christmas puddings because she never felt easy in her mind if they weren't made and safely put away by the end of August. As usual, each member of the family was happily getting on with his or her own affairs. Little did they guess how soon this state of things would be changed by the large new member who was going to erupt into their midst.

Sandy rolled onto her back to make sure that the twins were not climbing on slippery rocks or getting cut off by the tide. At the same moment a large body struck her forcibly in the midriff and she was covered by flying sand. Instinctively she shut her eyes and felt the sand being wiped off her face by something that seemed like a warm, rough, damp flannel. She opened her eyes and looked. It was a tongue. Its owner was a large and bouncy young Alsatian, or German shepherd, with topaz eyes, black-tipped prick ears, a thick, soft coat, and a bushy black-tipped tail.

"Lob!" shouted a man farther up the beach. "Lob, come here!"

But Lob, as if trying to atone for the surprise he had given her, went on licking the sand off Sandy's face, wagging his tail so hard while he kept on knocking up more clouds of sand. His owner, a gray-haired man with a limp, walked over as quickly as he could and seized him by the collar.

"I hope he didn't give you a fright?" the man said to Sandy. "He meant it in play—he's only young."

"Oh, no, I think he's *beautiful,*" said Sandy truly. She picked up a bit of driftwood and threw it. Lob, whisking easily out of his master's grip, was after it like a sand-colored bullet. He came back with the stick, beaming, and gave it to Sandy. At the same time he gave himself, though no one else was aware of this at the time. But with Sandy, too, it was love at first sight, and when, after a lot more stick-throwing, she and the twins joined Father and Don to go home for tea, they cast many a backward glance at Lob being led firmly away by his master.

"I wish we could play with him every day." Tess sighed.

"Why can't we?" said Tim.

Sandy explained. "Because Mr. Dodsworth, who owns him, is from Liverpool, and he is only staying at the Fisherman's Arms till Saturday."

"Is Liverpool a long way off?"

"Right at the other end of England from Cornwall, I'm afraid."

It was a Cornish fishing village where the Pengelly family lived, with rocks and cliffs and a strip of beach and a little round harbor, and palm trees growing in the gardens of the little whitewashed stone houses. The village was approached by a narrow, steep, twisting hillroad, and guarded by a notice that said LOW GEAR FOR 1 1/2 MILES, DANGEROUS TO CYCLISTS.

The Pengelly children went home to scones with Cornish cream and jam, thinking they had seen the last of Lob. But they were much mistaken. The whole family was playing cards by the fire in the front room after supper when there was a loud thump and a crash of china in the kitchen.

"My Christmas puddings!" exclaimed Jean, and ran out.

"Did you put TNT in them, then?" her husband said.

But it was Lob, who, finding the front door shut, had gone around to the back and bounced in through the open kitchen window, where the puddings were cooling on the sill. Luckily only the smallest was knocked down and broken.

Lob stood on his hind legs and plastered Sandy's face

with licks. Then he did the same for the twins, who shrieked with joy.

"Where does this friend of yours come from?" inquired Mr. Pengelly.

"He's staying at the Fisherman's Arms—I mean his owner is."

"Then he must go back there. Find a bit of string, Sandy, to tie to his collar."

"I wonder how he found his way here," Mrs. Pengelly said, when the reluctant Lob had been led whining away and Sandy had explained about their afternoon's game on the beach. "Fisherman's Arms is right round the other side of the harbor."

Lob's owner scolded him and thanked Mr. Pengelly for bringing him back. Jean Pengelly warned the children that they had better not encourage Lob any more if they met him on the beach, or it would only lead to more trouble. So they dutifully took no notice of him the next day until he spoiled their good resolutions by dashing up to them with joyful barks, wagging his tail so hard that he winded Tess and knocked Tim's legs from under him. . They had a happy day, playing on the sand.

The next day was Saturday. Sandy had found out that Mr. Dodsworth was to catch the half-past-nine train. She went out secretly, down to the station, nodded to Mr. Hoskins, the stationmaster, who wouldn't dream of charging any local for a platform ticket, and climbed up on the footbridge that led over the tracks. She didn't want to be seen, but she did want to see. She saw Mr. Dodsworth get on the train, accompanied by an unhappy-looking Lob with drooping ears and tail. Then she saw the train slide away out of sight around the next headland, with a melancholy wail that sounded like Lob's last good-bye.

Sandy wished she hadn't had the idea of coming to the station. She walked home miserably, with her shoulders hunched and her hands in her pockets. For the rest of the day she was so cross and unlike herself that Tess and Tim were quite surprised, and her mother gave her a dose of senna.

A week passed. Then, one evening, Mrs. Pengelly and the younger children were in the front room playing snakes and tadders. Mr. Pengelly and Don had gone fishing on the evening tide. If your father is a fisherman, he will never be home at the same time from one week to the next.

Suddenly, history repeating itself, there was a crash from the kitchen. Jean Pengelly leaped up, crying, "My blackberry jelly!" She and the children had spent the morning picking and the afternoon boiling fruit.

But Sandy was ahead of her mother. With flushed cheeks and eyes like stars she had darted into the kitchen, where she and Lob were hugging one another in a frenzy of joy. About a yard of his tongue was out, and he was licking every part of her that he could reach.

"Good heavens!" exclaimed Jean. "How in the world did *he* get here?"

"He must have walked," said Sandy. "Look at his feet."

They were worn, dusty, and tarry. One had a cut on the pad.

"They ought to be bathed," said Jean Pengelly. "Sandy, run a bowl of warm water while I get the disinfectant."

"What'll we do about him, Mother?" said Sandy anxiously.

Mrs. Pengelly looked at her daughter's pleading eyes and sighed.

"He must go back to his owner, of course," she said, making her voice firm. "Your dad can get the address from the Fisherman's tomorrow, and phone him or send a telegram. In the meantime he'd better have a long drink and a good meal."

Lob was very grateful for the drink and the meal, and made no objection to having his feet washed. Then he flopped down on the hearthrug and slept in front of the fire they had lit because it was a cold, wet evening, with his head on Sandy's feet. He was a very tired dog. He had walked all the way from Liverpool to Cornwall, which is more than four hundred miles.

The next day Mr. Pengelly phoned Lob's owner, and the following morning Mr. Dodsworth arrived off the night train, decidedly put out, to take his pet home. That parting was worse than the first. Lob whined, Don walked out of the house, the twins burst out crying, and Sandy crept up to her bedroom afterward and lay with her face pressed into the quilt, feeling as if she were bruised all over.

Jean Pengelly took them all into Plymouth to see the circus on the next day and the twins cheered up a little, but even the hour's ride in the train each way and the Liberty horses and performing seals could not cure Sandy's sore heart.

She need not have bothered, though. In ten days' time Lob was back—limping this time, with a torn ear and a patch missing out of his furry coat, as if he had met and tangled with an enemy or two in the course of his four-hundred-mile walk.

Bert Pengelly rang up Liverpool again. Mr. Dodsworth, when he answered, sounded weary. He said, "That dog has already cost me two days that I can't spare away from my work—plus endless time in police stations and drafting newspaper advertisements. I'm too old for these ups and downs. I think we'd better face the fact, Mr. Pengelly, that it's your family he wants to stay with—that is, if you want to have him."

Bert Pengelly gulped. He was not a rich man; and Lob was a pedigreed dog. He said cautiously, "How much would you be asking for him?"

"Good heavens, man, I'm not suggesting I'd *sell* him to you. You must have him as a gift. Think of the train fares I'll be saving. You'll be doing me a good turn."

"Is he a big eater?" Bert asked doubtfully.

By this time the children, breathless in the background listening to one side of this conversation, had realized what was in the wind and were dancing up and down with their hands clasped beseechingly.

"Oh, not for his size," Lob's owner assured Bert. "Two or three pounds of meat a day and some vegetables and gravy and biscuits—he does very well on that."

Alexandra's father looked over the telephone at his daughter's swimming eyes and trembling lips. He reached a decision. "Well, then, Mr. Dodsworth," he said briskly, "we'll accept your offer and thank you very much. The children will be overjoyed and you can be sure Lob has come to a good home. They'll look after him and see he gets enough exercise. But I can tell you," he ended firmly, "if he wants to settle in with us he'll have to learn to eat a lot of fish."

So that was how Lob came to live with the Pengelly family. Everybody loved him and he loved them all. But there was never any question who came first with him. He was Sandy's dog. He slept by her bed and followed her everywhere he was allowed.

Nine years went by, and each summer Mr. Dodsworth came back to stay at the Fisherman's Arms and call on his erstwhile dog. Lob always met him with recognition and dignified pleasure, accompanied him for a walk or two—but showed no signs of wishing to return to Liverpool. His place, he intimated, was definitely with the Pengellys.

In the course of nine years Lob changed less than Sandy. As she went into her teens he became a little slower, a little stiffer, there was a touch of gray on his nose, but he was still a handsome dog. He and Sandy still loved one another devotedly.

One evening in October all the summer visitors had left, and the little fishing town looked empty and secretive. It was a wet, windy dusk. When the children came home from school—even the twins were at high school now, and Don was a full-fledged fisherman—Jean Pengelly said, "Sandy, your Aunt Rebecca says she's lonesome because Uncle Will Hoskins has gone out trawling, and she wants one of you to go and spend the evening with her. You go, dear; you can take your homework with you."

Sandy looked far from enthusiastic.

"Can I take Lob with me?"

"You know Aunt Becky doesn't really like dogs—Oh, very well." Mrs. Pengelly sighed. "I suppose she'll have to put up with him as well as you."

Reluctantly Sandy tidied herself, took her schoolbag, put on the damp raincoat she had just taken off, fastened Lob's lead to his collar, and set off to walk through the dusk to Aunt Becky's cottage, which was five minutes' climb up the steep hill.

The wind was howling through the shrouds of boats drawn up on the Hard.

"Put some cheerful music on, do," said Jean Pengelly to the nearest twin. "Anything to drown that wretched sound while I make your dad's supper." So Don, who had just come in, put on some rock music, loud. Which was why the Pengellys did not hear the truck hurtle down the hill and crash against the post office wall a few minutes later.

Dr. Travers was driving through Cornwall with his wife, taking a late holiday before patients began coming down with winter colds and flu. He saw the sign that said STEEP HILL. LOW GEAR FOR 1 1/2 MILES. Dutifully he changed into second gear.

"We must be nearly there," said his wife, looking out of her window. "I noticed a sign on the coast road that said the Fisherman's Arms was two miles. What a narrow, dangerous hill! But the cottages are very pretty— Oh, Frank, stop, *stop!* There's a child, I'm sure it's a child —by the wall over there!"

Dr. Travers jammed on his brakes and brought the car to a stop. A little stream ran down by the road in a shallow stone culvert, and half in the water lay something that looked, in the dusk, like a pile of clothes—or was it the body of a child? Mrs. Travers was out of the car in a flash, but her husband was quicker.

"Don't touch her, Emily!" he said sharply. "She's been hit. Can't be more than a few minutes. Remember that truck that overtook us half a mile back, speeding like the devil? Here, quick, go into that cottage and phone for an ambulance. The girl's in a bad way. I'll stay here and do what I can to stop the bleeding. Don't waste a minute."

Doctors are expert at stopping dangerous bleeding, for they know the right places to press. This Dr. Travers was able to do, but he didn't dare do more; the girl was lying in a queerly crumpled heap, and he guessed she had a number of bones broken and that it would be highly dangerous to move her. He watched her with great concentration, wondering where the truck had got to and what other damage it had done.

Mrs. Travers was very quick. She had seen plenty of accident cases and knew the importance of speed. The first cottage she tried had a phone; in four minutes she was back, and in six an ambulance was wailing down the hill.

Its attendants lifted the child onto a stretcher as carefully as if she were made of fine thistledown. The ambulance sped off to Plymouth—for the local cottage hospital did not take serious accident cases—and Dr. Travers went down to the police station to report what he had done.

He found that the police already knew about the speeding truck—which had suffered from loss of brakes and ended up with its radiator halfway through the post-office wall. The driver was concussed and shocked, but the police thought he was the only person injured—until Dr. Travers told his tale.

At half-past nine that night Aunt Rebecca Hoskins was sitting by her fire thinking aggrieved thoughts about the inconsiderateness of nieces who were asked to supper and never turned up, when she was startled by a neighbor, who burst in, exclaiming, "Have you heard about Sandy Pengelly, then, Mrs. Hoskins? Terrible thing, poor little soul, and they don't know if she's likely to live. Police have got the truck driver that hit her—ah, it didn't ought to be allowed, speeding through the place like that at umpty miles an hour, they ought to jail him for life—not that that'd be any comfort to poor Bert and Jean."

Horrified, Aunt Rebecca put on a coat and went down to her brother's house. She found the family with white shocked faces; Bert and Jean were about to drive off to the hospital where Sandy had been taken, and the twins

were crying bitterly. Lob was nowhere to be seen. But
Aunt Rebecca was not interested in dogs; she did not
inquire about him.

"Thank the lord you've come, Beck," said her brother.
"Will you stay the night with Don and the twins? Don's
out looking for Lob and heaven knows when we'll be
back; we may get a bed with Jean's mother in Plymouth."

"Oh, if only I'd never invited the poor child," wailed
Mrs. Hoskins. But Bert and Jean hardly heard her.

That night seemed to last forever. The twins cried
themselves to sleep. Don came home very late and grim-
faced. Bert and Jean sat in a waiting room of the Western
Counties Hospital, but Sandy was unconscious, they
were told, and she remained so. All that could be done
for her was done. She was given transfusions to replace
all the blood she had lost. The broken bones were set
and put in slings and cradles.

"Is she a healthy girl? Has she a good constitution?"
the emergency doctor asked.

"Aye, doctor, she is that," Bert said hoarsely. The
lump in Jean's throat prevented her from answering; she
merely nodded.

"Then she ought to have a chance. But I won't conceal
from you that her condition is very serious, unless she
shows signs of coming out from this coma."

But as hour succeeded hour, Sandy showed no signs of
recovering consciousness. Her parents sat in the waiting
room with haggard faces; sometimes one of them would
go to telephone the family at home, or to try to get a little
sleep at the home of Granny Pearce, not far away.

At noon next day Dr. and Mrs. Travers went to the
Pengelly cottage to inquire how Sandy was doing, but the
report was gloomy: "Still in a very serious condition."
The twins were miserably unhappy. They forgot that

they had sometimes called their elder sister bossy and only remembered how often she had shared her pocket money with them, how she read to them and took them for picnics and helped with their homework. Now there was no Sandy, no Mother and Dad, Don went around with a gray, shuttered face, and worse still, there was no Lob.

The Western Counties Hospital is a large one, with dozens of different departments and five or six connected buildings, each with three or four entrances. By that afternoon it became noticeable that a dog seemed to have taken up position outside the hospital, with the fixed intention of getting in. Patiently he would try first one entrance and then another, all the way around, and then begin again. Sometimes he would get a little way inside, following a visitor, but animals were, of course, forbidden, and he was always kindly but firmly turned out again. Sometimes the guard at the main entrance gave him a pat or offered him a bit of sandwich—he looked so wet and beseeching and desperate. But he never ate the sandwich. No one seemed to own him or to know where he came from; Plymouth is a large city and he might have belonged to anybody.

At tea time Granny Pearce came through the pouring rain to bring a flask of hot tea with brandy in it to her daughter and son-in-law. Just as she reached the main entrance the guard was gently but forcibly shoving out a large, agitated, soaking-wet Alsatian dog.

"No, old fellow, you can *not* come in. Hospitals are for people, not for dogs."

"Why, bless me," exclaimed old Mrs. Pearce. "That's Lob! Here, Lob, Lobby boy!"

Lob ran to her, whining. Mrs. Pearce walked up to the desk.

"I'm sorry, madam, you can't bring that dog in here," the guard said.

Mrs. Pearce was a very determined old lady. She looked the porter in the eye.

"Now, see here, young man. That dog has walked twenty miles from St. Killan to get to my granddaughter. Heaven knows how he knew she was here, but it's plain he knows. And he ought to have his rights! He ought to get to see her! Do you know," she went on, bristling, "that dog has walked the length of England—*twice*—to be with that girl? And you think you can keep him out with your fiddling rules and regulations?"

"I'll have to ask the medical officer," the guard said weakly.

"You do that, young man." Granny Pearce sat down in a determined manner, shutting her umbrella, and Lob sat patiently dripping at her feet. Every now and then he shook his head, as if to dislodge something heavy that was tied around his neck.

Presently a tired, thin, intelligent-looking man in a white coat came downstairs, with an impressive, silver-haired man in a dark suit, and there was a low-voiced discussion. Granny Pearce eyed them, biding her time.

"Frankly . . . not much to lose," said the older man. The man in the white coat approached Granny Pearce.

"It's strictly against every rule, but as it's such a serious case we are making an exception," he said to her quietly. "But only *outside* her bedroom door—and only for a moment or two."

Without a word, Granny Pearce rose and stumped upstairs. Lob followed close to her skirts, as if he knew his hope lay with her.

They waited in the green-floored corridor outside Sandy's room. The door was half shut. Bert and Jean

were inside. Everything was terribly quiet. A nurse came
out. The white-coated man asked her something and she
shook her head. She had left the door ajar and through it
could now be seen a high, narrow bed with a lot of
gadgets around it. Sandy lay there, very flat under the
covers, very still. Her head was turned away. All Lob's
attention was riveted on the bed. He strained toward it,
but Granny Pearce clasped his collar firmly.

"I've done a lot for you, my boy, now you behave
yourself," she whispered grimly. Lob let out a faint
whine, anxious and pleading.

At the sound of that whine Sandy stirred just a little.
She sighed and moved her head the least fraction. Lob
whined again. And then Sandy turned her head right
over. Her eyes opened, looking at the door.

"Lob?" she murmured—no more than a breath of
sound. "Lobby, boy?"

The doctor by Granny Pearce drew a quick, sharp
breath. Sandy moved her left arm—the one that was not
broken—from below the covers and let her hand dangle
down, feeling, as she always did in the mornings, for
Lob's furry head. The doctor nodded slowly.

"All right," he whispered. "Let him go to the bedside.
But keep a hold of him."

Granny Pearce and Lob moved to the bedside. Now
she could see Bert and Jean, white-faced and shocked, on
the far side of the bed. But she didn't look at them. She
looked at the smile on her granddaughter's face as the
groping fingers found Lob's wet ears and gently pulled
them. "Good boy," whispered Sandy, and fell asleep
again.

Granny Pearce led Lob out into the passage again.
There she let go of him and he ran off swiftly down the
stairs. She would have followed him, but Bert and Jean

had come out into the passage, and she spoke to Bert fiercely.

"*I* don't know why you were so foolish as not to bring the dog before! Leaving him to find the way here himself—"

"But, Mother!" said Jean Pengelly. "That can't have been Lob. What a chance to take! Suppose Sandy hadn't —" She stopped, with her handkerchief pressed to her mouth.

"Not Lob? I've known that dog nine years! I suppose I ought to know my own granddaughter's dog?"

"Listen, Mother," said Bert. "Lob was killed by the same truck that hit Sandy. Don found him—when he went to look for Sandy's schoolbag. He was—he was dead. Ribs all smashed. No question of that. Don told me on the phone—he and Will Hoskins rowed a half mile out to sea and sank the dog with a lump of concrete tied to his collar. Poor old boy. Still—he was getting on. Couldn't have lasted forever."

"*Sank him at sea?* Then what—?"

Slowly old Mrs. Pearce, and then the other two, turned to look at the trail of dripping-wet footprints that led down the hospital stairs.

In the Pengellys' garden they have a stone, under the palm tree. It says: "Lob. Sandy's dog. Buried at sea."

Miss Spitfire

〰〰〰

"Put my bed out on the runway," Uncle Ned said, "for that's where I mean to die, and nowhere else."

Well, now, of course, this raised a whole set of problems.

"It's not respectable," Mum said, for a start. "Dying in public like that? Who do you think you are—King Charles the Second? What next, I should like to know? You might as well—" Then she went bright pink, and shut her mouth tight, and scowled.

"How are we ever going to *get* the bed there?" Dad said fretfully, and he looked from Uncle Ned's bed, which was big and sagging and had brass knobs wherever possible, to the bedroom door, which was of Tudor dimensions, only five feet high and two feet wide. Dad has a tendency to fuss over small details; it is his way of avoiding main issues.

"Bed got in here, it'll get out again, won't it?" snapped Uncle Ned. "Take it to bits, of course." He always had a forceful way with him, because he had been in charge of New Hibernian Airlines for twenty years, till his heart went bad on him and he took a fancy to come home and die in parts where he was born and brought up.

"What'll you do while that's going on?" Mum objected.

"Sit in a chair, or get into another bed. Or you can put a camp bed out on the runway. *I'm* not particular."

"Dr. Arden would never hear of such a thing," said my mother, seizing with relief on a likely let-out. "Why, you might get pneumonia out there."

"Don't be sillier than you were born to be, Martha," said Uncle Ned. "If my heart's gone bad on me, what does it matter if I do get pneumonia? Anyway, who ever heard of getting pneumonia in May?"

As a matter of fact, Dr. Arden, when he came, raised no objections at all to our putting a bed for Uncle Ned out on the runway. This was because, way back in their World War II R.A.F. days, when Uncle Ned was the youngest Wing Commander in Fighter Command, Doc Arden, who has no eyesight to speak of without his glasses, and never did have, had somehow winkled his way into ground operations, here at Chevron Hill, and the two men have been fast friends ever since.

There was a big house here before World War II, Chevron Hall, but one of the first German landmines smashed it to rubble, so they turned the place into an R.A.F. station and used the croquet lawn, which was a mile long, as a runway. Now it's a small commercial airfield and flying club. Dad, who was the gardener at Chevron Hall, lived in the West Lodge, and continues to do so. Only now it's market gardening.

Still and all, you will be wondering, if the airfield is in commercial use, why would Uncle Ned be allowed to have his deathbed put out on the runway? And the answer to that is that there was to be a two-day strike of air traffic controllers in support of some gripe about more adequate protection of air crews against hijackers. So for the next two days no aircraft would be flying about in the English sky; or, if they did, they would soon be in difficulties, because nobody on the ground would be looking after them.

"Mind you, though, old boy," said Doc Arden, taking my uncle's pulse. "Hmn, sounds like a bicycle with star-shaped wheels. Mind you, you'll have to get your dying done before Tuesday when they start up again. I don't say that's out of the question. But bear it in mind."

"Roger," said Uncle Ned. Roger is actually Doc Arden's name; the joke was so stale that it had turned funny again.

"Oh, dear," said my mother. "What the neighbors will say I do not like to think."

Doc Arden took no notice of that. "Have you a camp bed?" he asked. "If not I'll bring mine over. Helen's using it for sleeping in the garden, but she can stay indoors for a couple of days."

Helen is the doctor's daughter and my friend.

She and I took the bed out, unfolded it, and put it together right in the middle of the runway. And we made it up, nice and tidy, with two fat pillows and pink-and-white striped sheets and a thick Welsh blanket, blue and red and purple mixed. It looked fine.

"Ah," said Uncle Ned in a satisfied tone when he saw it. "That's wizard, that is. Piece of cake."

He doesn't really use R.A.F. slang anymore; from his grin we could see it was just to mark the formality of the occasion.

"Oh, Neddy!" lamented my mother, who, with Dad, had wheeled Uncle across the concrete apron in a chair borrowed from the Red Cross. "Must you really go on with this? Making yourself so conspicuous?"

"Who's to see?" says Uncle Ned, looking around him.

Chevron Hill is a big high hill in Hampshire; from it you get a view of the Isle of Wight and the Fawley oil refinery when the weather's clear, and if you look the other way you can see as far as the Chilterns, but there's nothing much in between, except a lot of larks singing their heads off and some cuckoos calling in the woods down below.

A lot of copper beeches grow in Hampshire. When the leaves are young, only just unfolded, they are the most amazing color, a bright dark-plum red. There were avenues of them all over the landscape. In between, explosions of flowering hawthorn. That was a great year for it; April and May were so cool and dry, the flowering season was longer than usual; all the hillsides and hedges were smothered in cascades of white blossom like birthday-cake decorations, or showers of white fireworks descending. And in among the red beeches and white mayflower and the green, green meadows, there were odd acres of mustard, dotted here and there. You know what color that is, when it's in flower—a pale, clear yellow; it doesn't half flash on a gray day when there's thunderclouds piling up in the sky. So the country was all red, white, yellow, and green.

Uncle Ned inspected all this landscape, which he was to see for the last time, and he looked even more satisfied. "I picked a good spot to die in," he says. "You can go back indoors, Martha, and watch television, or something. I don't want you moaning and whingeing around here, can't hear myself think."

"There isn't anything *on*, except the Open University!"

"Well, watch that, then, for Pete's sake. The kids can stay," Uncle Ned said, "so long as they behave themselves."

Well, Mum and Dad didn't like it, but they went; grumbled themselves off the runway again, dwindling into the distance with the wheelchair till they were as small as peas. Doc Arden had to visit a patient in Bishop's Tisted, so, after he'd seen Uncle Ned installed, with a ham sandwich, and a bottle of parsnip wine, and his transistor, and a hot-water bottle, the two men shook hands.

"So long, Roger."

"So long, Ned. Bombs away."

The doctor's little Mini went bowling down the runway, shining like a beetle in the stormy sunlight.

There we were, in the middle of nowhere, squatting by the camp bed.

"Uncle Ned," said Helen. (She is not really his niece, but had fallen into the habit of addressing him in this way because she has known him for so long.) "Uncle Ned, why exactly *do* you want to die out here?"

"Why," said Uncle Ned, sounding a bit surprised, as if he thought the whole world must know the story, "because of your father's sister, your Aunt Reine, of course."

"Aunt Reine? The one who was in the W.A.A.F.?"

"Of course," he repeated, and then lay with his hands extended on the purple-and-red blanket, looking a long way into the past.

His thoughts seemed very occupying, so, as we didn't want to disturb him with conversation, I turned on the transistor and found some music of the kind Uncle Ned likes—harpsichord pieces with names like The Knitters, and The Grape Gatherers, and The Mysterious Barricades. And we all three sat listening quietly.

After a while the music was interrupted for a news bulletin.

"Four German terrorists have hijacked a DC4 belonging to Turkish Airlines and are flying it north across Europe. They are demanding the release of some political prisoners held by the West German government. There are twelve passengers on board the plane, and the terrorists threaten to drop a passenger off the aircraft every hour until their demands are met. The DC4 is an unpressurized plane, so it is possible to open the cabin door while in flight."

Uncle Ned tut-tutted a good deal about that.

"The things these hijackers get up to! Dropping passengers out as if they were apple cores. Untidy. Inconsiderate too. Mind you, I've always said they ought to issue all passengers parachutes. Still, if I was the West German government, I wouldn't give in to 'em."

In order to distract him from this dismal subject, I said, "Tell about Helen's Aunt Reine, Uncle Ned? What did she look like?"

"Why," said Uncle Ned, "she was the spit of Helen here. Sleek and foxy. That's why I've always had such a soft spot for Helen."

So he had—and she for him. She'd have given the hair off her head to make him a pair of bedsocks. And the way they'd go on, ragging each other, you'd never guess there was forty years' age gap between them.

"Reine had pale-red hair, just like yours, Helen, lass," said Uncle Ned. "She wore it short, in a cap. Just the color of well-polished copper, it was. And she had gray eyes, and a pointed face, and a temper that you had to treat with respect. One thing that did make her fighting mad was that they wouldn't allow W.A.A.F. girls to fly. She'd got her license, she'd done well over a hundred hours, knew radio navigation and all that, probably better than some pilots that were up in the sky, but still those girls had to stay strictly on the ground. 'Oh, how I wish I could get up there and give those Huns a bash,' she used to say, shaking her fist at them when there were some Heinkels or Messerschmitts flying over. She used to work on me to take her up, smuggle her into my Hurricane, but I never would. There wasn't all that amount of room in a Hurricane, apart from everything else. All she was allowed to do was stay in the control tower and see we got up and down safe. She used to worry about me a fair old bit too, when the German bombers and their covering fighters were sweeping past in hundreds and the sky was as full of flak as a tin is of sardines. 'Don't you worry your ginger head about me, Lovey, I'll be all right,' I used to tell her. Somehow I always knew I would be. 'See you on the runway when I get back,' I used to say, and, as often as she could get out, when we got down, after fighting it out all night with the Heinkels, she'd be there. Give me a big hug, she would, ending in a fierce shake and saying, 'Why couldn't you take me with you, you mean so-and-so! One of these days I'll get up there somehow!' She never did, though. Miss Spitfire, they used to call her on the station. But I always called her Foxy."

Uncle Ned paused, with a sad, inward, reminiscent look in his eye.

"So what happened to her, Uncle Ned?" I asked.

"One evening I said 'See you on the runway,' and flew off. We had a big long fight over Reading that night, went on for hours. But when we came home we were diverted to Arunmere, because a Junkers 87, making for home, had dropped his last bomb on the Chevron Hill control tower. And there wasn't anything left of the tower, or the crew inside. It was Foxy who copped it, not me. And that's why I've a fancy to die out here on the runway—just in case she's waiting for me."

He looked around the hilltop. The sun gleamed even brighter, rays coming in very low and level, and the thunderclouds were piling up even higher; it seemed to me a fine place to die, and I thought Helen's Aunt Foxy might very well be waiting for him, and even getting a bit impatient. After all, it was some forty-one years she'd been hanging around, by now.

"When I'm dead," said Uncle Ned, "I want you to mind and make sure that your mum and dad do what I have expressed a written wish for—have me cremated and use my ashes in a practical way. Make them into an egg timer, or something of that sort."

"An egg timer, Uncle Ned? Wouldn't there be a good deal more ashes than you'd need just for an egg timer?"

"Well, then," he said, impatient, "put them on the garden, use them for compost, anything you like, just so's I don't have one of those droopy hypocritical funerals with everybody embarrassed, and saying a lot of things they don't mean and wouldn't have said while I was alive. Foxy didn't have a funeral, and I don't want one either."

I tried to imagine Mum timing the breakfast eggs with Uncle Ned's ashes, but my imagination couldn't make it any more than a camel could clear the jumps in the Grand National.

Uncle Ned took his own pulse. "Shan't be long now," he said briskly. "Just as well too, for it looks as if it's brewing up for a downpour in a brace of shakes. Too bad if your nice Welsh blanket gets soaked."

"Don't you worry about that, Uncle Ned," says Helen. "It'll dry."

"You kids had best get under cover," he said, and a rumble of thunder ended his words like a period.

The radio, which had gone back to music, gave a loud crackle, and then the announcer said, "The German terrorists on board the hijacked Turkish DC4 have carried out their threat and dropped out two passengers, one over Dijon and one over Normandy. But they are now in difficulties as they are running low on fuel and no French airport will allow them to land."

"Serve 'em right, stupid baskets," said Uncle Ned. "What do they expect, red carpet and a band playing the Marseillaise?"

There came another crack of thunder, and a big Z of lightning split the sky from top to bottom.

"Hop it, you two," said Uncle Ned. "That's all you need, to be struck by lightning sitting around my deathbed. Whereas it won't do *me* any harm at all." And he shook his fist at the heavens, as if inviting a thunderbolt, and bawled out, " 'Blow, winds and crack your cheeks!' Now give us a kiss, Helen, my love. You look so like your aunt that if it weren't for the age disparity—and Foxy waiting for me up there—I'd have married you and now you'd be setting up to be a widow. So things are best as they are. So long, young Ted," he said to me, and shook my hand. "Don't take any bent pennies. And keep an eye on Helen, there. And mind what I said about the ashes. Run, now!" as another lightning flash zipped across the sky and the rain began to come down like steel needles.

So we ran—getting drenched on the way across to the canopy where passengers were supposed to wait for their planes on a fine day—when there were any planes to wait for.

There we stayed. You could just see Uncle Ned, tiny in the distance; his bed looked about the size of a head of purple clover. And the rain came lashing down on it in gray torrents; and every now and then the wet concrete glittered in a flash of lightning.

"Your mum'll be out pretty soon with an umbrella, if this goes on," said Helen, "I'm surprised she hasn't been out already."

But my mother hates thunder; she unplugs the TV and sits with a bathtowel over her head.

Every now and then Uncle Ned would give us a wave—we could see the blue flash of his pajama sleeve—to show us he was still alive and enjoying the storm, which certainly did him proud for a deathbed sendoff; it went on and on, scissor-flash of lightning followed close behind by a cracking roar of thunder.

"It's lucky we made that hot-water bottle good and hot," said Helen.

"And that there was a whole pint of parsnip wine," I said.

Then we began to hear a rumble that wasn't thunder.

"That's funny," Helen said in a troubled tone. "Sounds like a plane—but how could it be? There aren't any planes about."

But there was a plane.

In a few minutes we saw the big dark shape, ghostly in the dimness, big because it was flying very low, groping its way among the thunderclouds. It drew in, lower and lower, circling round.

"Oh, *no!*" I said in frozen, disbelieving horror. "It's going to come down! But how can it land here? There's nobody in the tower to give it permission—"

"And what about Uncle Ned?" croaked Helen.

She was holding on to my arm as if it were a lifebelt; her fingers dug right in. She gave a sudden gasp. "Look —look at its markings! There's some Arabic writing— and a crescent—"

Next minute the plane touched down. And as it did so there was another terrific flash of lightning, which seemed to split the carriage clean in half. The rear half of the aircraft toppled off the runway onto the grass at the far end. The front half went on, careering along toward Uncle Ned with flames pouring up and back from it, like a torch on rollerskates. Just as it reached his bed, the whole thing went up in one cataclysmic explosion, sky high.

A lot of people were soon on the spot. Of course the explosion had been heard for miles around. Doc Arden was the first, because he had been driving back up the hill in his Mini and saw the whole thing.

He helped Helen and me get ten passengers out of the rear half of the plane. They were dazed, shattered, sick with fright, but not much hurt except for a few bruises. Two of them spoke some English. One of these was a middle-aged woman. She seemed sensible enough.

"The *extraordinary* thing," she said, "was this girl who suddenly came out of the galley. Wearing some kind of uniform—but she wasn't a stewardess. None of us had known she was on the plane. She went forward to the cockpit, where the hijackers were, and told them they could land here, she knew this field. She'd land it for them, she said. And then she ordered the rest of us to get to the back of the plane, where she said we'd be safe. She was English, I think. And—and then she went along to the front of the plane again."

"What did she look like?" asked Helen.
"Why—she looked very like you, my dear."

There wasn't a chance of turning Uncle Ned's ashes into
an egg timer; how could we have told which they were?
But we didn't think he'd really mind.

Finders Keepers

~~~~~

Halfway through the spring term we always have a school trip to the museum at Strand-next-the-Sea. Strand is the nearest town to our school, Candlemakers, which is not far from a village called Far Green. Far Green can hardly be called a place—three houses and a pond; in World War II they moved the school from London to a big red Victorian drafty hulk of a mansion here, thinking it would be safe from bombing because the Germans would never see it. In fact it's so hard to see that visiting parents often get lost and end up in Staithe Cross or Watchett. The house is in the middle of a kind of miniature forest: elms packed tight around it like insulation. A lot of the elms got Dutch disease, so they look like gloomy old skeletons, but then a whole grove of young sycamores shot up among the elms.

Apart from the trees around the school, it's flat, windy country. From the spire of Far Green church you're supposed to be able to see Norwich, in clear weather, if you look one way; and if you look the other way, in foggy weather, you're supposed to be able to see the spire of

Losthope Minster, which vanished under the sea in the great gale of 1609.

The spring term is always dismal. Wind rages in across the North Sea and rain pours down five days out of six; the games fields are generally under water, and so it's cross-country jogging, day after gusty, drenching day. By midterm, although Strand is a bleak little town and the museum is simply three rooms of rubbishy odds and ends collected by some nineteenth-century reverend who had nothing else to do with his spare time, everybody is quite pleased to go there. At least it's indoors, under cover. We go there by school bus, and it makes a bit of a change; though of course by the time you have been at the school a few years, you know everything in the museum as well as the contents of your own desk.

This term I'm speaking of there was a new boy called Denzil Gilbert. He was a thin, pale-eyed, spotty character with a rough skin like sandpaper and a slight squint in his left eye, so that you never knew whether he was speaking to you or to somebody over your shoulder. Nobody liked him much, but that didn't seem to bother him; he was wonderfully self-satisfied and would talk away endlessly about himself to anybody who cared to listen. A lot of the stories he told were just plain lies: that his father had won the Nobel Prize for poetry and his grandmother was a famous actress who had played Lady Macbeth with Sir Henry Irving, his grandfather was Lord Chancellor of England and his family had come to England with the Normans. Anybody who could be bothered to check in Who's Who or the encyclopedia would find that most of his tales just weren't so, except for a tiny grain of truth somewhere at the bottom. By the middle of the term nobody took much notice of his boasting.

Denzil was the kind of character who, because he was

not interesting in himself, always took care to have rather uncommon possessions, so that he could show them off and get a bit of prestige that way. He had a set of Maundy money—a tiny silver penny, and a twopenny, three-penny, and fourpenny piece; he had a metal powder horn studded over with bits of turquoise and red coral, which he said had belonged to King James I (though in my opinion, if James I had a powder horn, it would be a fancier-looking article than Denzil's); he had a fossil that he said came from Mars; and a big cowrie in which you were supposed to be able to hear the Indian Ocean roaring; and a little soapstone inkwell that (according to Denzil) had belonged to an old Chinese poet called Li Po, and anyone who used it would be able to write top-class Chinese poetry. And he had a Malay kris, and a piece of rose quartz, and a leaf from a Handkerchief Tree, and a lot of nice old green marbles.

People laughed at Denzil's stories about his possessions, of course, but they were interested and used to ask to look at them, and he was always pleased to display them; and before long—you know how it is at school—especially if a person is rather unpopular—several of the things went missing, in particular the set of tiny silver Maundy money pieces. Denzil was very upset about that. They had disappeared from a tiny silver snuffbox that he kept on his chest of drawers in his dormitory.

Of course Jasper, the headmaster, got to hear about it, and he made a statement after prayers and asked if any-body knew where they were. No one said a word. Jasper was very angry—partly with Denzil, because he said the top of a chest of drawers was a stupid place to keep something so valuable, it was putting unfair temptation in people's way. And the end of it was that a new rule was made: all valuables had to be handed in to Sally Lunn, the matron. So Denzil had to part with his quartz and inkwell, though he was allowed to keep the cowrie and the Martian fossil, because nobody believed they were what he said.

It was all awkward and uncomfortable, and didn't make Denzil any more popular, as you can imagine.

One thing he was good at, though, was telling ghost stories, when classes were finished and we were all huddled around the dining-room stove; or at night after lights out. Then he'd have everybody's hair standing on end with tales of the drowned Danish warriors caught by the tide on Saltwagon Marsh after they had been deliberately misdirected by a village boy; the dripping-wet Danes rise up, he said, out of their muddy graves on the last night of May and go looking for that boy to have their revenge, so watch out! And there was another good story about the sunken forest of Losthope, and the awful forest Things that come slithering out, sometimes, in winter gales, when the waves are so huge, up and down, that stumps of the rotted, fossilized trees can still be seen. Or so it's said. And there was a story about giant African bees, moving northward through Europe, in black crowds a million strong, killing everything on the way.

But none of the stories Denzil Gilbert told us was any stranger than what happened to him.

On this particular Saturday Sally Lunn announced at breakfast that we'd be going to Strand-next-the-Sea museum after lunch, and all the people who'd been there four or five times before gave their usual groan of boredom. But Denzil looked quite bright-eyed and keen. Biddy Frazer was so rash as to ask why. I was surprised, because she was generally one of the first to snub him;

she was Scottish, and down to earth, and a monitor, and said his stories were silly rubbish.

Denzil said, "My father was born in Strand-next-the-Sea. Our old family house is there."

"Then why aren't you a day boy?"

Biddy's tone was wistful. Hours less of Denzil every day, she was plainly thinking.

"My grandfather sold the house. And we've always lived abroad. My father's professor of English at Addis Ababa University." This was true; one of the things Denzil hadn't invented.

After lunch the rattly old blue bus trundled onto the gravel turnaround in front of the main schoolhouse, and we all splashed out through the rain and climbed on board, with the usual moans and grumbles and ribald jokes about where we'd rather have been going.

Nobody wanted to sit with Denzil, so he ended up sitting by Tom Oakenshaw, the English master, who could be very sarcastic but was still being fairly patient with Denzil, as he was a new boy, and prepared to listen to his tall tales without too obvious an expression of disbelief.

The old bus went plowing along the flat marshy roads, throwing up sheets of water, under the huge gray wet windy sky. I was sitting behind Denzil and Oakie, and could hear Denzil shooting a line about his family.

"The Gilberts have lived in Strand-next-the-Sea since the twelfth century."

"I'm not certain that Strand was there in the twelfth century," said Oakie mildly. "The sea was farther out then, you know."

"Oh, well, my family have been in these parts since then, anyway," said Denzil, making a quick comeback. "Some of them went on crusades from here. There was an ancestor of mine buried in Losthope Minster—Sir Geoffroi de Guilbert; there's a picture of his monument in a book called *Lost Curiosities of East Anglian Architecture.*"

"Really?" says Oakie. "I have that book back at school. I'll look up your ancestor when we get back."

Biddy, beside me on the seat behind, was stifling her laughter and giving me pokes because she was ready to bet that none of Denzil's story was true and Oakie would soon find that out. But Denzil seemed quite calm about it.

Presently we rolled into the main square of Strand, which was always a windy, unwelcoming place. One of the four short, wide streets led straight to a row of ever-shifting sand dunes; another went to the harbor; one had some shops in it; and the fourth had private houses, the church, and the museum.

"Museum first," said Oakie. "Then you can spend your pocket money and have a run on the beach, if it isn't raining too hard."

We all slouched, two by two, along Staithe Street to the museum, which was in a red-brick Georgian building called Acre House. As soon as Denzil arrived in front of it he struck a dramatic attitude and exclaimed, "The home of my ancestors!"

Most people sniggered, and Oakie hustled us inside.

As I said, there are three rooms. One is full of old agricultural and kitchen utensils, plows and churns and butterpats and clothes wringers. The metal things are rusty and the wooden ones are worm-eaten, and unless you are a history enthusiast it's pretty boring.

Another room has a lot of stuffed birds, and local plants growing in tubs, and a big geological scale model of the country round about; that's the room I like best.

The third room has clothes and costumes, and a huge

old dolls' house, and newspapers left over from the eighteenth century. Most of the girls spend the whole visit in there.

Biddy went off to the costume room, after whispering to me that she was going to faint in ten minutes. Biddy is pale and red-haired, and she is able to make herself faint by putting blotting paper in her shoes and then concentrating very hard. She doesn't do it too often, or the staff would get wise to it, but this time she said she'd seen Acre House often enough, and she wanted to spend the birthday money her mother had sent. If she fainted, she said, we might be allowed to go and have tea at Polly's Plat, the only café that stays open through the winter.

Denzil went straight into the costume room, and I wandered in there, after five minutes or so, because I wanted to watch Biddy stage her faint.

Old Miss Thorpe was doing her stuff. She is the curator; she looks like a lichee nut, pinkish brown and wrinkled. She must have read about a million books, because she can lecture on and on endlessly about every single object in the museum.

"This is a pilgrim's costume," she was saying. "You see the cockles or scallop shells on the hat—they show he went to the shrine of St. James at Compostela. And the piece of palm shows that he went to the Holy Land too. The hook on the staff was for carrying his bag.

"Now, here we have the costume of a crusader. He wore banded mail, a white surcoat to keep off the hot sun, and, as you see, the surcoat has a red cross on it. These are the clothes of Sir Geoffroi de Guilbert, whose family lived at Gippesvicum—that's Ipswich—and whose descendants built this house in the eighteenth century."

"See!" squeaked Denzil proudly to Jane Hall, who

happened to be standing by him. "Didn't I say this was the home of my ancestors!"

Miss Thorpe turned around at that, very interested. "And what may your name be, my boy?"

When he said it was Denzil Gilbert, she was as pleased as Punch.

"The son of Professor Robert Gilbert? Now, isn't that perfectly splendid! I've never had a member of the family in the house before."

As you can imagine, Denzil just stood there looking like the rising sun. For once, a story of his had proved to be true, and you could see it would be a long time before he would let us forget it.

But Miss Thorpe hadn't finished yet.

"As you're a member of the family," she went on, "you may exercise the privilege of *filius donationis*—this has never happened yet during the time I have been in charge here, what fun, how topping!" When Miss Thorpe becomes excited she tends to slip into Boys' Own Paper language, vintage 1920.

"What is *filius donationis?*" inquired Mr. Oakenshaw, almost as interested as the old girl herself.

"Why, when the house and various bits of property that went with it were presented as a museum, it was a condition of the agreement that if ever a descendant of the donor—Sir Giles Gilbert—"

"My grandfather," sang out Denzil happily.

"If ever a descendant of Sir Giles came in, he might be allowed to handle the articles in that locked case over there."

All heads turned, and all eyes focused on the locked case, which was not very big, and had various small dull objects in it—chains and buckles and seals and coins and links and some dingy little spoons.

Denzil was not going to pass up a chance like this, of course.

"Can I handle the things, please?" he said.

"Certainly, you can, my boy. Just a moment while I fetch the key."

Denzil peered through the glass, looking horribly self-important; and as many people as cared clustered around to have a look too.

"There's something written on the spoons—it's in Latin," said a girl called Tansy Jones.

"Probably the Latin for 'A Present from Norwich.'" Bill Humphrey sniggered.

"*Dona ex Norvicio*," suggested Jane.

"No, it isn't," said Miss Thorpe, returning with the key. "Those are Roman silver spoons, found on the site of a temple to Faunus, the wood god. Faunus, as you may know, is also the British god Vaun and the Greek god Pan —the letters *V*, *F*, and *P* are all interchangeable." Miss Thorpe was well into her stride now.

"What do the words mean?" Tansy asked.

"Something like 'Rejoice in the woods.'"

"Have a nice picnic," muttered Bill.

"All this country was covered by forest at that time, of course. The temple site is where your school now stands. Now, these are little bits of Roman glass," said Miss Thorpe, handing them to Denzil, who tried to look interested but found it hard going. "And these are ancient British arrowheads. And this little thing has a curious history—it's called the Finder."

It was a small metal image of a stocky, smiling little man with a lot of hair and beard, wearing a pointed cap. His feet were backward-way on.

"Why the Finder?" asked Denzil.

"Because it is supposed to help find lost things. It is an image of the forest god Faunus—or Vaun."

"Why should he find lost things?"

"Why—I suppose—because things often *are* lost in the woods. In Roman or British days the lost article would probably be children—or dogs or pigs or cattle—and they believed that if you sacrificed to Vaun he would help you find what you had lost. Then later, instead of sacrificing, people began having these little images made and giving them to the temple. This one was dug up in the seventeenth century by a farmer, and it was given the name of the Finder because, even then, people believed it had the power to find lost things. It was passed from hand to hand all over the district, and in the end it fell into the keeping of your great-great-grandfather Sir Neville Gilbert," Miss Thorpe told Denzil.

"I jolly well wish it was mine," he said. "It's just what I need."

This was the moment Biddy chose to stage her faint. She did it very artistically, going paper-white, swaying to and fro, then falling on the wood floor with an almighty thump.

"Oh, bless my soul!" said Miss Thorpe, hastily locking the glass case and sticking the key in her cardigan pocket. She and Oakenshaw hoisted Biddy up and dumped her on a wide old leather couch in the front room, and after a minute she opened her eyes, looked around in a dazed way, and said:

"What happened? Where am I?"

"Just lie still, dear, and I'll fetch you a glass of water," said Miss Thorpe.

"I'd rather a cup of tea," said Biddy.

"Why don't I take her to Polly's Plat?" I suggested.

But, very annoyingly, Oakie wouldn't let her go to the

café. He said she was too groggy to be walking about, and she must sit quietly in the bus while the rest of us spent our pocket money. He escorted Biddy out to the bus and left her in the charge of the driver, Gus Beadle, who never bothered to get out but just stayed on board reading the *Sporting Times.*

Biddy gave me money to buy her a chocolate mint bar and I went off to the one sweet shop. Denzil tagged along with me. He was still looking as pleased as a dog with two tails, I supposed because of all the attention he'd been getting.

I collected a couple of coffee crisps and Biddy's chocolate mint bar, then waited at the counter behind an old character who was buying a packet of pipe tobacco and some extra-strong peppermints. He was feeling about in all his pockets and seemed upset; in fact, he had gone almost as white as Biddy.

"What's up, dad?" said the girl at the cash register.

"Lost me five-pun' note," said the old fellow. "Oh, drabbit me, what can I have done with the blame thing? I dunno what my old woman'll say—"

"It's under your foot," said Denzil quietly, as the old man peered hopelessly about the cluttered little shop.

Sure enough, there the note was; he must somehow have pulled it out of his pocket without noticing and then stepped on it after it fell. Was he relieved!

He paid for his things, and I bought my stuff, and Denzil got some marshmallows, sickly things—I suspected he bought them because nobody else liked them, so he wouldn't have to give any away; then we walked back to the bus. By now the drizzle had hardened to a steady downpour, given extra zip by a sharp north wind; it was certainly no day for strolling along the sand dunes.

Denzil and I were the last two back on the bus. I

handed Biddy her chocolate mint bar. She was sitting by Oakie, looking sorry for herself, so white that her freckles stood out like rust spots. In fact, I began to wonder if perhaps it had been a real faint.

Gus Beadle started his engine, but before he could pull away the bus door flew open. The gale had blown up tremendously fast, as it does in these parts; one minute it's dead calm, five minutes later chimney pots and roof tiles are sailing down the road.

"Shut the door, will you, Bill," called Oakie.

Bill, who was next it, thumped it to, but it blew right open again. In the end Gus had to tie it shut with a bit of cord, and Bill had to hold on to it all the way home. The old bus itself nearly lifted off the road, every now and then. It was a real force ten.

Denzil sat by me. He was smirking away to himself still, and once gave me a poke in the ribs and muttered, "I say! Shall I tell you something?" But I pretended not to hear. I was listening to Oakie, in the seat ahead, who was talking to Biddy and a couple of other girls about the Finder.

"An archaeologist called Murray Parkin borrowed it from the museum eight or nine years ago. He hoped it might help him find a Saxon treasure ship like the one at Sutton Hoo."

"Did it?"

"Not that I ever heard. Unless he went off with the treasure! Perhaps it doesn't work if you borrow it. The seventeenth-century belief was that it had to be given, or stolen."

"Maybe over the last three hundred years its power got weak from lack of use," suggested Jane Hall. "Like a flashlight battery."

"Somehow I don't think that would happen." Oakie

took her quite seriously. "I feel it would be just the other way round. The power would get more and more concentrated. Vaun—Faunus—was a forest god. Quite wild, quite strong. What do you suppose it feels like, if you are a god, not to be worshiped? To have people forget you— ignore you? For hundreds of years?"

"Not very nice, I should think," said Tansy.

"It would make you angry," said Jane. "Especially if, when people did remember you, all they wanted was for you to find their lost Aberdeen terrier—"

Biddy shivered and said in a whining tone, "I do feel rotten, Mr. Oakenshaw! My head aches, and I'm freezing—"

"You're probably coming down with the flu," he said. "You must go straight to matron as soon as we get back."

It began to seem a wonder that we got back at all. The elms and sycamores around the schoolhouse were thrashing about as if they were likely to come clean out of the ground, and when Bill undid the bit of cord the bus door flew open so violently that it crashed against the side of the bus and cracked a window. Oakie and I helped Biddy out. She was shivering and looked green rather than white; the sight of her made me feel a bit queasy too.

The rain was slamming down, so we all bolted into the house. And then we couldn't get the front doors to stay shut. They are two big double ones, heavy oak and iron strapping; the wind kept sucking them open as if they were made of cardboard. Oakie and old Gus had to lock and bolt them before they would hold, and even then they rattled and swayed as if a dinosaur were battering them.

Sally Lunn led Biddy off to the sick bay.

"Can't I go to my room first and get a book?" asked Biddy.

"No, you come with me. One of your friends can bring you a book later," said the matron.

The rest of us went in to tea—it is always chocolate swiss roll on Saturday.

Denzil plumped himself down by me.

"Hey! Look what I've got!" he said, showing me something quickly in the palm of his hand.

I had only a hasty glimpse of it but it looked uncommonly like the little black Finder.

"*Christmas!*" I said. "You don't mean to say you've gone and pinched the—"

"Shhhh! Not so loud. I haven't pinched it."

"I never heard you ask old Thorpe."

"I'll return it—maybe," he said smugly. "Just as soon as it's found my lost things for me." He gulped down the last of his tea. "Come on—want to see it work?"

I didn't, actually; the whole thing gave me a nasty feeling. And the weather didn't help; it was much darker than it should have been at that time of the afternoon; the wind outside was making a continuous howl like a chain saw, and doors kept bursting open all over the building.

"Old Jasper's going to be sick as a dog if he finds out what you've done," I said. "Stealing from a museum."

"Oh, don't be such a prig!" said Denzil sharply. "Besides, I have a right to it. It belonged to my great-great-grandfather."

"And how do we know how *he* came by it?"

Denzil simply walked out of the big dining room and up the stairs, cupping the little black thing in his hand.

"It's leading me," he said.

Very unwillingly, I went after him, and so did two or

three other people, who had got wind somehow that queer business was afoot.

"Look, *honestly,*" I said, shouting to make myself heard above the howl of the wind, "I don't think you ought to do this. It's bound to lead to trouble. And—did you hear what Oakie was saying on the bus—if you use this—this kind of thing—you are laying yourself open to forces that —that are better kept separate. It's like touching a live wire. You are putting yourself in its power—"

"Oh, bunk," said Denzil. "You don't want me to do it because you're scared of where my things are likely to turn up." He gave me a nasty grin, looking over his shoulder—as always, I couldn't be sure if his eyes were on me or on someone else. "I wonder why *that* is," he said, and kept on going. "It wants to go higher up."

He climbed the next flight of stairs, which led to the girls' dormitories.

"Hey! You're not supposed to go into other people's rooms," said Tansy, who was tagging along behind. Denzil ignored that. He went into the big room that Biddy Frazer shared with Jane and two others. Nobody was there. One of the windows burst open as Denzil walked in, and all the cubicle curtains streamed sideways like banners. A shower of postcards and paperback books blew off the tops of dressing tables.

I struggled to shut and latch the window, and Tansy tried to sort out the cards and put them back where they came from.

Denzil had walked straight to Biddy's corner of the room. A photograph of her family hung on the wall over the bed. He lifted the frame away from the wall, and down fell a thick envelope that had been lodged behind it. Inside were Denzil's little silver Maundy pieces—the penny, twopenny, threepenny, and fourpenny.

"I thought as much!" he said in a satisfied voice.

"You utter beast! You knew they were there!" exclaimed Tansy. "Or else you put them there yourself. What a stinking rotten trick. I don't believe Biddy took them."

"Oh, yes, she did," said Denzil, gloating. "And now I'm going on to find the rest of my things—the powder horn and the Malay knife and my green marbles."

He looked round at us all, and his smirk was very unpleasant.

"Who'd have thought that Biddy would be the one to take the coins—being a monitor, and so goody-gum-drop, setting herself up to be better than everybody else. Won't old Jasper be surprised when he hears!"

"You'd better go to him now," said Jane, very troubled. "In case—in case suspicion is resting on the wrong person."

"I'll tell him all right, by and by," said Denzil. "Not yet, though."

"Why not?"

"What, and give the people who took my other things a chance to put them back? Not likely!" And he grinned again, an ugly grin.

Then he looked down again at the little black thing in his hand.

"Vaun, Vaun, little god of the woods," he chanted, "help me find my powder horn and my Malay knife and my green marbles."

At that moment a voice was heard calling.

"Denzil! Denzil Gilbert! Are you up there?"

"He's up here!" called Jane. "Who wants him?"

"He's wanted down below."

Afterward none of us could agree whose voice we had

heard; Jane thought it was Jasper, I thought it was Mr. Oakenshaw.

"Oh, blow," said Denzil. He tucked the Finder into his pocket, with the Maundy money. "Well, I'll go on with the hunt in a minute; you had all better wait for me here, if you want to watch."

He started down the stair. "I'll just go in here," he said, and turned into a bathroom that was to the side of the staircase, one step up. He shut the door, and Tansy said:

"Quick! Hadn't we better tell old Jasper what's going on? He won't like it a bit, and he'll be certain to blame us as well—and if we tell him, he'll take the Finder away from Denzil before—"

Just at that moment we heard Denzil, who was still inside the john, give the most extraordinary cry—a kind of howling wail, as if all the breath were being sucked out of his lungs. At the same moment the gale sucked a lot more doors and windows open. The whole building seemed to rock to and fro, and a couple of elms crashed down outside.

"What's up, Denzil?" I called, rattling the door handle. "Are you okay?"

But there was no answer from inside the john.

In the end we had to get Oakie and Gus Beadle to break down the door. And that was the strangest moment of all, for Denzil wasn't inside. That john had a tiny round window like a porthole. A well-fed cat couldn't have got through it. And it was five floors up. But Denzil wasn't there, and we never saw him again.

A memorial service was held for him, nine months later, when he was presumed dead.

During the service I was beside the slab erected to

Denzil's great-great-or-whatever-it-was-grandfather. So I had plenty of time to read the verse on it, which said:

> Liste to the winde's lamente
> Take heede of its dreare sounde
> O Man! Seeke not to finde
> Lest ye yourselfe be founde!

"This tablet was erected to the memory of
Sir Giles Gilbert,
who dyed very suddenly in the 65th yeare
of his age, February 27, 1753."

The Finder, which was discovered on the bathroom floor, was returned to the Strand museum and locked up again in the glass case by Miss Thorpe. The Maundy money was not found, but Denzil's clothes and other things were sent off to his parents. The green glass marbles and Malay knife never turned up. And I buried the powder horn under the elm trees one windy night. It seemed the best thing to do with it.

The Windowbox Waltz

~~~~

Rosemary lay stretched and baking on the sunny beach, watching a boat unloading. It was a foreigner—unusual in the small Cornish harbor—with an unpronounceable name, full of *s*'s and *v*'s, and manned by blond Nordic sailors with peeling, sunburned noses. There was a woman with them too, also tall and blond, with the figure of a goddess in her fitted coveralls and a face like the bottom of a frying pan, squashed and sour under the golden plaits. She seemed to have authority among the men, who treated her with respect.

A whistle blew, and the creaking and thudding of machinery stopped; peace fell over the harbor and Rosemary almost drifted off to sleep under the noon sun. Then, irritating as a mosquito, came a sound from above. Footsteps walking to and fro, to and fro, on the harbor wall above her, and not talk that she could have ignored, but a thin persistent whistling that repeated again and again a tinselly little theme—pom *pom* pom, pom *pom* pom, pom tiddle om pom, om pom pom—that was vaguely familiar, and after a few repetitions she identified it as a tune from early piano lessons called the "Windowbox Waltz."

In exasperation she screwed her head around and looked up. It was the pan-faced Vikingess, strolling on the harbor wall with a man in bottle-green corduroys; presumably having run out of conversational topics, he was whistling to her to fill in the gaps and he seemed all set to go on till two o'clock.

Rosemary had discovered an excellent method of shifting people if she wanted them out of the way: it was to start taking photographs aimed in their direction; nice-minded people always hurried self-consciously away for fear of getting in the picture and spoiling it. Accordingly she scrambled up the sandy steps and leveled her camera at the strolling couple.

She was not prepared for what happened.

The woman gave a sharp exclamation; the man broke away from her, strode over to Rosemary, grabbed the camera, and threw it into the deep water of the harbor.

He and Rosemary stared at one another.

"What the dickens do you think you're doing?" she exclaimed furiously.

"I do not care to have my picture taken by strangers," he replied harshly.

"Do you realize that camera cost fifty pounds?" Rosemary said. "It's my father's. You'll have to replace it!"

"I don't care if it cost a hundred pounds. You have no right to take my picture."

"I haven't the slightest wish to take your picture! You don't improve the view of the cliffs at all. Will you please give me your name and address, unless you happen to have fifty pounds on you?"

The harbor policeman strolled toward them. Rosemary turned to him in relief, but the man spoke first.

"This young woman is annoying us," he said. "She seems to think she can get money out of me with some cock-and-bull story of a camera, but she is mistaken. Will you please caution her, or whatever you do?"

"Oh!" exclaimed Rosemary, bursting with rage, but the policeman turned calm, oxlike eyes from one to the other.

"He threw my camera into the harbor!" Rosemary exploded. "It was worth fifty pounds."

"Fifty pounds? That's a likely story," the policeman said. "What were you doing with a camera worth that?"

"It's my father's. And I'm a photography student."

"I did see something chucked in," the policeman said.

"I threw in a stone," the man cut in. "Isn't that so?" he appealed to the woman.

"*Ja,*" she replied stolidly. "He throw in a stone."

"It's two against one, miss," the policeman pointed out heavily. "After all, what would the gentleman want to do a thing like you said for?"

Rosemary turned and called to a man who was sprawled on a beam of timber above them a little way up the cliff path.

"Can you come down a minute please?"

Grinning, the man joined them. He was dark, dressed disreputably, and had a sardonic expression.

"You saw him throw my camera into the harbor, didn't you?" Rosemary asked him. "You must have, you've been here all along."

"Nope. Didn't see a thing," said the man with complete calm.

"You—you absolute so-and-so!" Rosemary exclaimed. Her temper got the better of her and she smacked his face. It was not logical, but it made her feel better.

"Now, now, dear," the man protested, grinning still

more. He put an arm around her and said to the policeman, "I must apologize for my young sister. She's a bit
temperamental—thyroid gland trouble. Nothing to
worry about, she'll soon be all right."

With a little bow to the group he led Rosemary, quite
bereft of speech, along the dusty harbor to a small green
sports car. He deftly insinuated her into it, slid into the
driver's seat, and drove rapidly up the steep winding
road until they were on the height of the cliffs and out of
sight of Polbissick Harbor.

There he pulled up.

"Now, have a good cry, why don't you," he suggested
mildly. "It'll help."

"Have a good cry—" She faced him with stormy eyes.
"Do you know you've lost me a—"

"Yes, I know, I know," he said soothingly. "I've probably saved your life, while you've just cost me six weeks'
work—probably irreplaceable."

"Saved my life? What on earth do you mean?"

"Quite simple. If you'd stayed there, pestering that
bloke for your fifty pounds, the odds are about a hundred to one that in the next few hours you would have
been overtaken by some nasty accident—a hopper full of
cement would have landed on you, or you'd have tripped
and fallen under the boat, or, simpler still, he'd have
taken you off in his car to settle the matter at the nearest
lawyer's and you'd never have been seen again."

"You can't be serious?" Rosemary said. "Who is he?"

"His name's Peterson."

"Carl Peterson, I suppose?" she said witheringly.
"Why not Dr. No?" She still thought he was joking. "I
suppose you're James Bond?"

"No, seriously, he's a very dangerous man. Do you live
around here?"

"I'm on holiday, staying with my aunt Lou. She has a bungalow above Linhoe."

"I'll run you back. You're better at home while he's around."

"But who is he? What does he do?"

"I'd have found out a bit more, but for your interruption with the camera. I was just getting close enough to lip-read when you had to butt in."

"You wouldn't have heard anything. They weren't talking," Rosemary said. "He was only whistling a tune."

"*Was* he?" said the man with extreme interest. "You wouldn't remember it?"

"Yes, I do, as a matter of fact. I used to play it. It's called the 'Windowbox Waltz.' " She whistled it.

"You wonderful girl! That's well worth a new camera. Do you suppose if I rang up my boss in London you could whistle it to him? I'm tone-deaf," he confessed. "Old Waterfalls would never have put me on the job if he'd known music was going to come into it."

"I expect I could. Are you really not pulling my leg? Are you from Scotland Yard? What's your name?"

"Alan Hawthorne. I've been seconded to the Yard from the Ministry of Defence—" and then suddenly he leaned nearer and hissed, "Don't look round, but he's followed us up here and he's sitting in his car watching us."

Rosemary fished out the mirror she kept in her skirt pocket. Holding it at a cautious angle, she surveyed the car behind. There was a gleam as something metallic inside it caught the sun, and Alan let out a soft curse.

"There's an old Home Guard slit trench over to your left in the heather," he said. "Make for it, wriggle along it on your tummy—it runs all the way to Linhoe—and when you get there, if I'm not about, ring up my boss,

Westminster nine thousand, and whistle that tune to him. Say Peterson's here. Okay? Ready?"

He was holding her hand tight. She stared at him in fright, wondering what he meant to do. He levered himself swiftly out of the car, there was a slight whirr, as if a hollow golf ball had buzzed past them, and Alan toppled neatly forward over the sloping edge of the cliff and disappeared from view.

The whirr sounded again. Something like a hornet brushed past Rosemary's ear. She felt sick, but plainly this was not the moment for standing about and pondering. She flung herself sideways out of the car into the slit trench, which was about four feet deep. The heather had grown right over the top.

Rosemary lay still, her face on some dusty old dry sand and a weather-beaten cigarette packet. She was terrified of adders and imagined them thudding down on to her back out of the heather, larger than boa constrictors, but even so, they seemed preferable to Peterson and his airgun, or whatever it was.

There was no sound from above, however, and after a while she plucked up courage and began inching along on knees and elbows. The going was soft but not pleasant; sharp bits of dead heather pricked her, and once she had to negotiate a dead sheep. After what seemed a mile of crawling, she cautiously put up her head and found she was out of sight of the road. There was no sign of Peterson, and just below was the cliff path, curving temptingly through the heather. She made her way down to it and ran on toward Linhoe.

By this time she was in a considerable rage. It is always a shock when an acquaintance is shot in your presence, even if it is someone you have not known long. Rosemary's knees were knocking together slightly, her heart was beating more than her steady jog trot justified. She certainly intended to see Peterson brought to justice, and that sourfaced blonde too. The first thing would be to visit the police station, before calling up Alan's boss, to make sure the pair were arrested before they left the neighborhood.

The police station was at the top of Linhoe Hill, opposite the Coast Guard post. There was a mirror just inside the door, and as she went in Rosemary caught a rather demoralizing glimpse of herself—hair like a haystack, a scratched face, and hands stained with sand.

"I want to report a murder," she said abruptly.

A couple of men were lounging in the little room. One was skillfully darning a sock on an old-fashioned wooden darning egg, the other was thoughtfully reading a comic, his tongue laboriously moving from side to side.

"Top Cat's stuck inside the dustbin," he said. "Proper job." Then he raised his head and added, "Eh? What was that?"

"I've come to report a murder," said Rosemary crossly. "A man was shot by another man who's just thrown a fifty-pound camera of mine into Polbissick Harbor."

"Who'd carry a camera weighing fifty pound?" said the other man.

"Cost, not weighed," snapped Rosemary.

"Where did this happen?"

"On the cliff above Polbissick."

"Then how could he have thrown the camera into the harbor?"

"We'd gone there afterward."

"After what?"

"After he'd thrown the camera in, of course!"

She turned just in time to see the man who had been

reading the comic lick his finger and pass it across his forehead with a loud, expressive hiss.

The other policeman looked at her compassionately. "You've got a touch of the sun, miss," he said. "High temperature, shouldn't wonder. Lie down on that bench for a minute, and we'll make you a nice cup o' tea. Then you can tell us the whole story, at your leisure, like."

Rosemary looked at them exhaustedly. They did not believe her. People don't shoot one another and throw cameras into harbors. Sunstroke is much more common.

"You'll find his car," she said, remembering. "It's at the top of the cliff, and his body'll be somewhere at the bottom, if the tide hasn't washed it away."

They began to look more intelligent.

"Young Harry could go along on his motorbike when he comes back with the toffee," the comic-reader suggested. "That won't do no harm."

"You wait here in the cool, miss, till he comes," they told her.

"Could I make a phone call?"

"Surely, surely. It's on the wall behind you."

"London, Wesminster nine thousand," Rosemary said into the old-fashioned mouthpiece. There was a long pause while the names of distant towns linked together between her and London: then a snappish female voice was asking her which department she wanted.

All at once Rosemary realized that she didn't know the name of Alan's boss.

"I—I want to speak to someone high up," she said doubtfully.

"What division?"

"It's a division that a Mr. Hawthorne works in."

"No Mr. Hawthorne on our list," announced the voice after a pause, and Rosemary remembered with a sinking heart that Alan was seconded from some other ministry. "What did you want to speak about?"

"I—I wanted to leave a message from Mr. Hawthorne."

"What was the message? Perhaps I could identify—?"

"It was a tune."

"A tune? I'm sorry. I can't help you. I think you must have the wrong number."

"It went like this," said Rosemary despairingly, and began whistling. A click told her that the operator had hung up.

She turned to see that this conversation had revived all the policemen's doubts. One had brought a bottle of aspirin out of a drawer while the other was hastily thumbing through the first-aid book for sunstroke.

"The man who did the murder," Rosemary told them earnestly, "is tall and dark and rather fat and wears green corduroys and suede shoes."

"Yes, yes," they soothed her. "We'll catch the miscreant, no danger. Soon as Harry gets back with the toffee."

Rosemary glanced out of the door and her eyes bulged. Walking leisurely down into Linhoe was Peterson himself.

"There he is!" she hissed to the two men. "Look! He must have left his car behind in the car park at the top."

Disbelievingly they crossed to the door, but of course by the time they reached it Peterson had turned the corner out of sight. Rosemary darted after him. The two policemen looked after her for a moment, then returned to their occupations.

"Daft," said the elder one. "Daft as my sister Aggie's youngest."

Rosemary ran down into Linhoe, but to her dismay

Peterson had vanished, and though she scoured the High Street, there was no sign of him.

Tired, dispirited, and at a loss, she turned into a snack bar, had a sandwich and some coffee, and tidied herself up. What to do now? Go back to the police? And then, as she stood indecisively in the street, out of a first-floor window came the familiar notes of a tune: "Pom pom—pom tiddle om pom—" It broke off abruptly and the player switched to "The Blue Danube."

Rosemary stopped, as if her head had been pulled up by a string. There was a door beside her and a flight of outside steps; a notice said that this was Madame Brzofska's Academy of Dancing. Rosemary ran up.

She came to a small lobby, and then to a large bare room, with a polished floor and hard wooden chairs round the walls. Twelve little girls in frilly organdy dresses were dancing with bamboo pipes while a row of parents sat dismally at the end of the room.

Rosemary put on dark glasses, as the best she could do in the way of disguise, and looked about her. The woman who had been playing the piano stood up and glided toward her. She had pale eyes like marbles, a receding chin, and a bun.

"You must be Miss Bugge, our new pianist," she said with a cross smile. "You are late. Please sit down and begin."

If I must I must, Rosemary thought, and she sat down at the piano while Madame Brzofska darted to the little girls, who had been taking a breather.

"A polka now, Miss Bugge, and I want to see some beautifully pointed toes—like *this.*" Rosemary obediently began playing the next piece in the book, "The King Pippin Polka." Madame Brzofska tripped back and forth, her toes, in their strapped black patent shoes, pointed like daggers, her navy silk skirt held up to reveal chiffon underskirts in puce and cyclamen.

"*Point*, Cecily!" she cried. "Toes should point *down*, not up. Arms, Prudence—beautifully curved, like a willow. Tum, tum, tara, tum, tum. Nicely, Jacqueline. Cecily, your toes! Again, Miss Bugge."

As Rosemary began "The King Pippin" again she felt somebody behind her and, turning her head slightly, saw with tightening breath that Peterson had come in.

"Ah, Dr. la Poer," said Madame Brzofska, swimming toward him. "Delightful to see you here!"

"I have come with your tickets for tonight's concert," he said affably. "Seven o'clock in the town hall. But perhaps I may be permitted to stay and watch?"

"Of course! Now, children, your pipe dance—very beautifully, please, as dear Dr. la Poer is watching. I want to see a row of graceful little fountains, little waterfalls. Miss Bugge, 'The Windowbox,' please."

Rosemary jumped, flipped over a page, and began playing "The Windowbox Waltz" while the children once again began skipping round with their bamboo pipes.

> *"I've a bungalow deep in the jungle-oh*
> *For my true love turned out to be false . . ."*

Something Madame Brzofska had said was fidgeting Rosemary's mind, and it took her a moment or two to realize that the waltz was arranged for four hands and she was playing one part only.

"I will assist you," announced Peterson, and he drew up a chair beside her and swung into the sugary rhythm of the waltz.

Rosemary was fairly sure he had not recognized her—one mouse-fair girl is very like another—and the glasses helped, but this close proximity made her feel very ill at ease.

All at once, under pressure from her overstrung nerves, perhaps, she remembered what Madame Brzofska's words had recalled. "A row of little waterfalls," she had said, and Alan had spoken of his chief as old Waterfalls—of course! If only she could get away to a telephone. Could one ring up a ministry and ask for old Waterfalls?

Her right hand banged into Peterson's left as they negotiated an arpeggio, and he hit a wrong note. Suddenly she realized that he was staring at her hand, on which she wore an opal ring, set in a silver butterfly. Rosemary cursed inwardly.

His eyes met hers.

"Enough, thank you, players," sang Madame Brzofska, swooping toward them with a toothy smile. "Rest for a moment, children, and then we will practice our tango."

A buzz of voices broke out as the children stacked their pipes on the piano.

"They would do for blowpipes, would they not?" said Peterson pleasantly in Rosemary's ear. He picked up one of the pipes, and, still smiling, still keeping his eyes on her, he pulled a little case out of his vest pocket, remarking, "South American poison-arrow darts. No use at long range but invaluable in emergencies like the present and quite undetectable. I never travel without them."

Rosemary glanced around frantically. Madame Brzofska was at a distance, talking to the parents. Peterson started to open the case.

"Cecily, come here, dear," called Rosemary. "Your elastic must have broken." With a startled look the child obeyed, and Rosemary, suddenly springing up, twitched the case from Peterson's hand, dodged behind Cecily, and ran out of the door, slamming it. She turned the key in the lock and flung it and the case of darts into a garbage truck that chanced to be passing in the street below, before running down the steps.

She guessed her start would be short. There must be more than one exit to the hall. Peterson would be after her in a moment, so she ducked into the first door she came to.

It was a hat shop with the name Gwendolyn in trailing gilt letters.

"I'd like the pink jersey cap and scarf, please," Rosemary said boldly, hoping she had enough money.

Looking into the mirror when she had put them on, she exclaimed, "Heavens, I look like Yul Brynner."

"It's a lovely color, isn't it?" the girl said. "Just suits you."

It certainly changed Rosemary's appearance.

"Have you a phone I could use?" she asked as she paid the fearful price.

There was one in the little office at the back. As she picked up the receiver Rosemary had the satisfaction of seeing Peterson pound furiously past down the street.

"Westminster nine thousand?" she said into the mouthpiece. "Which division do I want? Oh"—putting on a high girlish giggle—"tee-hee, could I speak to old Waterfalls, please. Oo, I'm ever so sorry, it slipped out, I *should* say Mr.—er—"

"Mr. Torrence?" said the switchboard girl. "I'm putting you through now. . . ."

The concert in the town hall was evidently to be a grand affair. The posters advertised songs and ballads by well-known local artists and—the main attraction—a violin recital by a famous Russian artist accompanied by the

High School Parnassus Band (percussion and strings) conducted by Dr. J.S. la Poer, who had a string of musical honors after his name.

Old Waterfalls had told Rosemary to keep strictly out of the way, but it was more than flesh and blood could bear; she could not, simply could not, resist turning up to see what would happen. After all, didn't she owe it to Alan to see his murderer caught?

She slipped in unobtrusively by a side entrance, bought a cheap ticket, and found herself a little seat overhanging the orchestra platform. The singers and small orchestra were already in position. Rosemary looked around hopefully for signs of Waterfalls' men, who, he had promised, would be plentifully there. Perhaps that large man in the front row with his hat on his knees was from the Special Branch?

Peterson appeared, in tails, with his hair slicked down, bowed deeply to the responsive audience, and the concert began.

A large woman (whom Rosemary recognized as one of the dancing-class mothers) advanced to sing some well-loved ballads.

First she sang "Ben Bolt," drawing out the long notes until the echoes came back from the liver-colored marble figures of Justice, Plenty, and Civic Pride on the walls and hit her. The audience throbbed in sympathy.

Then she sang:

> *"The boy I love is up in the gallery*
> *The boy I love is looking down at me*
> *There'e is, cantcher see, waving of 'is ankerchee,*
> *'Appy as the robin that sings in the tree."*

Up to this moment Rosemary had not noticed there was a gallery, but now, looking up, she saw another large mass of people overhead. And, surely, wasn't there somebody waving a handkerchief in the shadows?

The next song was ushered in by a resounding *clang* from the cymbals: the pianist played an introduction that was by now tolerably familiar to Rosemary, and the large woman, taking a hefty breath, proclaimed in her powerful contralto:

> *"I've a bungalow deep in the jungle-oh*
> *For my true love turned out to be false*
> *Though he swore that one day he would fetch me*
> *away*
> *As we whirled in the Windowbox Waltz."*

Rosemary kept her eyes glued on the gallery. More waving. It must be a code. But who was signaling, and to whom? And were Waterfalls' men in the hall, and had they seen it?

A clang from the cymbals heralded the chorus, and Rosemary's paper bag of sandwiches fell to the floor. She stooped for it.

> *"But he left me a wallflower from that day to this*
> *And I sit in the jungle and hear the snakes hiss*
> *But as long as I live I'll remember his kiss*
> *As we whirled in the Windowbox Waltz."*

Clang! went the cymbals again, and this time Rosemary's scarf fell off the arm of her seat. Retrieving it, she noticed a neat, slightly scorched hole clean through it. Now she noticed that there was another such hole in the paper bag; in fact, somebody was shooting at her under cover of the noise of the cymbals, and unless she moved before the next *clang* she was a dead duck.

She slid rapidly to the left, treading on the feet of the whole row.

Gaining the shelter of a pillar, she looked back just as the next *clang* fell due and saw Peterson pointing his baton, which, she now observed, was a neat, slender little gun, in her direction. *Slam!* went the cymbals in a triumphant finale, a chip flew off the pillar, and Rosemary darted out into the passage, to be grabbed by two unmistakable plain-clothes policemen.

"I'm not the one you want!" she snapped. "The conductor's been shooting at me. And someone's signaling in the gallery."

They gazed at her doubtfully.

"That's as may be," said one. "Someone else'll take care of them. There's one being brought down now."

And in fact Rosemary saw with consternation that her aunt Lou was being escorted down by two more burly men.

"I kept waving and waving at you, dear," said Aunt Lou placidly. "Didn't you see me?"

"What are you doing here?" Rosemary asked, wondering if she was going mad.

"Oh, that's a long story, dear. However, it will have to wait."

And indeed Aunt Lou disappeared between her guardians before Rosemary could protest, and the only mitigation was the sight of Peterson at the end of the passage in the midst of a mass of dark-blue uniforms, complaining and gesturing wildly. Rosemary tried to see more but one of her guides drew her away with a firm hand, saying, "Mr. Torrence said I was to put you on the bus, miss, and see you stayed there, and that you was to go home and not come out again tonight."

"But my aunt? What about her?"

"I don't know about that, miss. I daresay she'll be along by and by."

He escorted her to the double-deck bus, and Rosemary took a seat downstairs, with hauteur, but feeling rather like a small child who has been sent home early from a party in disgrace.

The bus had moved off, but was still not at full speed, when there was a sound of running feet and a man flung himself on the platform.

"Single to Polbissick," he said, and Rosemary's heart sank as she recognized the voice of Peterson. How in heaven's name had he managed to escape the posse in the town hall?

He came and sat behind Rosemary, who felt like Miss Muffet. She said to the conductor, "I'm going upstairs, I want to see the view," and climbed swayingly to the top deck, which was empty and extremely stuffy. She made her way forward and shoved down one of the side windows to its fullest extent. Then a brilliant and simple plan for escape struck her. The bus was just starting its long, low-gear climb up Linhoe Hill, inching along between twenty-foot banks crowned with a thickset holly hedge. The road was so narrow that every now and then the holly squeaked and rattled on the windows on the left-hand side.

Rosemary acted before she had time to lose her nerve: she stood on the seat, stooped, clutched the sides of the window, wriggled her head and shoulders through, held on tight, and somehow forced the rest of her body out through the narrow space. Turning around and letting go all in one movement, she launched herself against the hedge, which was only a foot away. She gasped as she hit it, and shut her eyes; a thousand holly spines seemed to be sticking into her face, neck, arms, stomach, and legs; she wondered if Peterson's blowpipe wouldn't have been preferable.

But she hung on and heard the bus go up the hill without her, reach the top, and change gear. She thrust painfully through the hedge at a weak point, and came out bleeding, torn, and raveled, lacking a shoe and the pink hat, her skirt more or less in rags.

Luckily Aunt Lou's bungalow was only ten minutes' run across the fields. There was no sound as she went through the gate. The place seemed dark, silent, and empty; the curtains were drawn; the key was under the mat.

But when she had let herself into the dark hall she saw a strip of light under the kitchen door.

Rosemary hesitated—could Aunt Lou have got home first?—and then went in.

Alan was sitting snugly in front of the kitchen fire with one leg, heavily bandaged and splinted, stretched before him on a stool.

The sight of him was so totally unexpected that Rosemary had to steady herself against the doorpost.

"Hi, there, clever girl," he said, grinning.

"Alan! Is it really you?"

"Didn't your aunt tell you?"

"She didn't have a chance. Police were dragging her away."

"Oh, dear, they always make such a mess of things. But it'll sort itself out. I rely on your aunt. When I crawled in on knees and elbows she set my leg and treated me for shock like a professional; I needed it too, after dangling on that cliff under an overhang till Peterson thought I must have been washed away. And then she went off to the concert to see the doings."

"But how did you know about the concert?"

"Because as soon as I got here I rang my office. You, with remarkable efficiency, had already got on to Torrence, squads of special branch police were streaming down in helicopters, and your aunt, who seems to know your character well, said she'd better go to find you and make sure you weren't getting into trouble. Torrence will bring her along when he comes to collect me. Did they get Peterson?''

"No, that's the awful thing," said Rosemary, sobering; she told Alan how Peterson had escaped.

"We must phone Torrence at once."

But when she tried it, the telephone was dead.

Rosemary had become used to the cold clutch of fear, but this time, perhaps because she was tired, perhaps because of the presence of Alan, injured and unable to walk fast, she felt numb from head to foot with an awful certainty. The dark fields stretched around the house, the sea washed below, and the nearest help was three miles off.

She imagined the conversation between Peterson and the bus conductor.

"Who's the young lady? Oh, that's Miss Hoylance's niece, staying with her at Moon Cottage, over the fields yonder. This is her stop—funny, she don't seem to be coming down. . . .''

She had made a muck of it. How long would it be before Alan was fetched? Where was Peterson now?

Pretending cheerfulness, she went back to the kitchen and said, "The line's engaged. I'll try again in a—"

"Don't move."

Such a quiet voice.

Rosemary's heart gave a violent bang and her fingers clenched the table's edge. Alan's eyes slowly lifted and he looked past her.

"Mr. Peterson," he said gently.

"So I didn't finish you off after all?" Peterson strolled

forward to warm himself at the hearth while he continued to keep them covered with his little gun. "You are an
enterprising pair. It is sad that I have to kill you."

"Why do you?" said Rosemary crossly. "It won't help
you. You've already been identified."

"Identity is nothing. Dr. la Poer will cease to be and
Julius Mendes, bass flutist, will take his place." He smiled
complacently. "No, I am killing you out of revenge, for
spoiling my beautiful system. Now: I have only two shots
left, so stand quite still, please. . . ."

Several hours later the police arrived. They had
wasted a good deal of time searching for Peterson in the
town hall after he got away, and were pleased to find him
ready for them, neatly bound and trussed. Rosemary said
acidly, "We might have been dead long ago for all your
help."

"How is it that you're not?" inquired her aunt inter-
estedly, handing round cups of tea. "Sugar, Mr. Hawthorne? I've given you the invalid's cup."

"Alan squirted spray furniture polish all over him as
he was trying to shoot us. That's why he has a glassy look.
And I hit him with a saucepan and we tied him up."

Aunt Lou looked regretfully at a broken mirror and
windowpane.

"That's the lot, then," the local superintendent said
cheerfully as Peterson was escorted out to the police van.

"I still don't know what it was all about," Rosemary
complained to Alan.

"Shall I tell you a secret?"

"Yes!"

"Nor do I."

"Oh," she said. "Well, do you think your ministry will
give me a new camera?"

"I should think so."

"Do you know," she said, starting to laugh, "I've thought of something. Peterson needn't have chucked it in the harbor. I'd forgotten to wind the film after the last shot."

The Swan Child

~~~~~

My brother and I decided we'd do a sponsored walk of our own. We didn't want to go with the others to Midchester Priory; we wanted to go to the Swan Child on Abbotsbury Hill. It was nine miles off, so if we managed to get there and back, that would be eighteen miles. Our uncle Christy Thorpe keeps the pub at the foot of Abbotsbury, so he'd sign our card saying we really walked there, and our planned route was all paths across country, so there'd be no question of cheating and accepting lifts from motorists.

Well, we went all around the village collecting sponsors. Five pence a mile, most of them offered; one or two went as high as ten. The money was to be spent on books for the school library.

The last house in the village, at the far end from ours, Nash End House, is a big square white one. We know Mrs. Williams, who lives there, because she helps in the school library once a week. Beyond her house there is an orchard, then a marshy field, then the Bungalow, all by itself in a clumpy overgrown garden, backing against a piney hillside. About the people who lived in that house we knew nothing at all. They didn't mix in village affairs.

"Who *does* live in the Bungalow?" Jake asked Mrs. Williams when she was signing our form. "Are they weekend people?"

"Oh, I wouldn't go there," she said hastily. "Some very odd people live in that little house. I've seen a couple of women, and there used to be a man—but I believe he died, I haven't seen him for a long time. . . ."

"How, odd?" I asked.

"Well, sometimes I've heard somebody laughing in a crazy way, on and on—and, once or twice, screaming. They never seem to come out. No, I'd advise you to skip the Bungalow if I were you. You seem to have got everybody else in the village," she said, looking at our list. "Have a good day. You've got fine weather for it, anyway. Enjoy yourselves on Abbotsbury Hill."

We *had* got all the rest of the village, and, just because of that, it was annoying not to have the Bungalow as well. We went rather slowly past the garden gate, which was an ordinary white-painted split-paling one, rather in need of a new coat of paint, tucked in between two big feathery clumps of bamboo. A garden path inside led to the one-story slate-roofed house, which was covered with trellis and clematis. On either side of the path were high plants —tiger lilies, and rosebushes, and phlox. All seemed peaceful and ordinary enough.

"Oh, come on," said Jake. "Let's chance it. They can't eat us. And we can always run like maniacs and scream bloody murder if they come after us with axes."

So, our hearts going pit-a-pat, we opened the gate and went in, tiptoeing up the path, across which lay a tangle of garden hose. We were about halfway along it when a voice stopped us in our tracks.

"Hullo?" it said—quite normally and pleasantly, but it came from behind us, which was somewhat disconcerting. "What do you want?"

We spun around. And there was a woman sitting on a stool in the middle of a little patch of lawn to our right, painting a picture on an easel. She wore a striped cotton dress and sandals and a big shady hat. "I'm Clarissa Forbes," she went on, quite friendly. "What can I do for you?"

There was a narrow grassy alley that led to her patch of lawn between the clumps of flowers, so we went along it, and Jake, who is a year older than me, explained about the sponsored walk, while I looked at the picture on the easel.

It was a picture done in watercolors, of the flowers in the garden, but not realistic: the plants were drawn out into long straggly spindly shapes, all twined in among one another, in odd but clear colors, very bright, very dark, with hard lines in between; and somewhere in among the twisting wreathing stems you could just see a person, who might have been partly a plant or else caught among them and struggling to get out. It looked as if it must have been painted very fast and skillfully— some of the color was still wet. I thought it marvelous— the shapes and colors seemed just right, and they gave you a feeling of excitement and satisfaction at the same time, as if it were not what you had expected, but now that you saw it you realized it was what you had been wanting all the time.

"Do you like it?" Clarissa Forbes asked, noticing that I couldn't take my eyes off it.

"Oh, yes, I do! *Very* much!"

"Good," she said, writing down 10 pence on Jake's

form. "When I have done enough of them I'm going to have a show."

"Have you done many?" I asked, longing to see more and hoping that she'd offer to show them. I began to study her carefully. Her face looked worn but smooth, like a stone that has been under water. Her eyes were big, wandering, pale blue, she wore no makeup, and her hair, a mixture of fair and gray, was bundled into an untidy knot. She was very, very thin; I noticed that her wrists were thinner than mine and there was a scar on one. She wore some kind of foreign sandals on rather dirty bare feet.

"Oh, yes, I've done hundreds. I hardly do anything else, really. Only," she said, looking around vaguely, "I'm not sure where they are. I can never lay my hands on them when I want them." She smiled a little, looking at her hands, which, oddly enough, were in cotton-mesh gloves, perhaps because several of her fingers seemed to be bandaged. I supposed the gloves would keep the bandages clean. "Where are you going on your walk?" she asked us.

Jake told her, Abbotsbury Hill, to see the Swan Child. The Swan Child isn't really a swan child. It is a chalk picture, where the grass has been cut away on the side of the hill to show the white stone beneath, very old, done in the Iron Age. It could be a swan or a kneeling person with head down and arms extended. If you stand on the bare chalk where the lines of its two arms, or wings, cross each other, you are supposed to have your wish granted, whatever that is.

"The Swan Child," said Clarissa Forbes. "Oh, I've heard of that! Oh, I *wish* I could come with you!" She sounded really wistful and envious.

"Well, why don't you?" said Jake. "It's only nine miles.

Or, if you don't want to walk so far, you could go by road, if you have a car. That's a bit farther."

"No," she said. "We do have a car, but I don't drive. The others can, but they wouldn't care about seeing the Swan Child. No, I'm afraid I can't come. But I do wish I could." She did sound sad.

Everything she said was perfectly ordinary, and yet there was something odd about her. I liked her—and felt sorry for her too—but I could see that Jake was itching to get away. There was a very oppressive, shut-in feeling about the little garden with its high bamboo hedges all around and the pine woods beyond, and the clumps of tall, gaudy flowers. Jake, turning, stumbled over more of the tangled hose, which led in from the main path; one end stuck out of the lawn and part of it was buried underground, which seemed slightly peculiar; maybe it led to an underground valve.

"Where does it go?" I asked.

"I'm not sure," Clarissa said vaguely. "One of the others would have to tell you that."

From the way she said "the others" you'd think the place was packed with people, but there wasn't a sound or a sign of anybody else; it was dead quiet.

"Well—thanks very much," Jake said, making rapidly for the gate.

I hesitated, and said, "Shall we call in on the way back —supposing we manage to get all the way to the Swan Child—and collect the money?"

She looked anxious.

"What time would that be?"

"Oh—around six, I should think. We're not likely to be back before then."

Her face grew even more anxious.

"Then I think you'd better not. If it was well before six —that would be all right. But—"

"Oh, never mind. If you're likely to be out, we'll call back some time next week," Jake called back quickly.

"No, it's not that. I never go out. But, you see, at six, or thereabouts, I change into one of the others. They don't realize I know that, but I do!" she said, laughing. "And they wouldn't like to see you *at all*—either of them. So it would be better if you came in the morning some time— I'm always here then."

Change into one of the others? I wondered what on earth she could mean.

"Come on, Cis!" called Jake, already on the other side of the gate. But Clarissa went on, in a confidential tone.

"You see, there are three of us. Originally there were four. But now it's Esme, Ag, and me." She laughed again and said, "They think I am very silly—the baby of the family. Head in the clouds. Well—Esme *is* very capable, of course. She's our organizer. And Ag is the servant. They don't like children, I'm afraid. Or anybody coming to the house, really. So, whatever you do, don't come here after six. Neither of them would give you any money, whichever you saw. And there might be trouble."

"*Cis!* Do come on, or we'll never get there!" Jake shouted impatiently from the road. So I hurriedly said good-bye and ran out and joined him.

"Please make a wish for me on the Swan Child!" Clarissa called after me.

"What shall I wish?"

But Clarissa merely sighed.

"*Broo!*" said Jake, as we started along the path through the pinewood. "What an old spook! I couldn't stand her. She gave me the cold hab-dabs."

"She'd painted a terrific picture," I said. "I liked that. And I felt sorry for her."

"Well, I didn't! I don't care if I never see her again. I vote we don't bother about collecting from her. Doesn't sound as if we're likely to get the money. And we've enough without."

"That seems a waste."

"She probably hasn't any money."

"What *can* she have meant—about changing into one of the others?"

"I don't know and I don't care!"

But all day I couldn't stop thinking about it.

That was a long, hot walk. We trudged along footpaths, and around the edges of plowed fields, over stiles, through copses, over sandy headlands of heath; we crossed brooks by plank bridges and squelched our way through soggy water meadows; once or twice we had to cross a main road or make use of its bridge to get to the other side of a real river. Jake had the map and steered us along; he is good at that; and we could see our general direction easily enough, because there, ahead of us, was the line of hills, with Abbotsbury higher, head and shoulders above the rest. As we came closer we could see the Swan Child above us, a swirl of white, mysterious lines on the pale-green hillside.

Uncle Christy gave us apple juice to drink in the pub garden, which was just flat, trampled grass and rustic seats; all summer long he had so many customers that there was no time for gardening. It was very different from the airless, shut-in garden of the Bungalow, with all its clumps of sultry-smelling lilies and bamboo.

"You'd best go up the hill before you have your lunches," Uncle Christy told us. "You won't be so keen after. And it's a steep pull. Hop along now, and I'll have a plowman's lunch ready for each of you when you come down.''

So, feeling a bit stiff already after our short rest, we went on up the steep chalk track. You could see all the flat country laid out down below, dark blue-green woods and hedges, pale yellow-green wheatfields in between them. Above us the sun baked down, hotter and hotter, and the hillside smelled of thyme. In a way I would have preferred rain and mist and the place to ourselves; when we got up to the Swan Child we found about twenty people having their picnics there and taking photographs—well, it was a Saturday, of course, you had to expect crowds. I waited my turn, and stood on the bald spot where the Swan Child crosses her wings, and wished that I would be a great painter when I grow up, that my name would be known all over the world like Picasso's. Then I remembered that Clarissa had asked me to wish a wish for her, so I tried to wish a blank wish and hold it inside me like a bubble unbroken.

I had a feeling that if I could get it back to her still unbroken, she would be able to use it.

Jake stood on the cross too, rather quick and embarrassed as if he thought it childishly beneath him to do such a thing. I didn't ask what he wished, because you mustn't, but I guessed that it would be connected with learning to fly, which is his one aim and ambition. In spite of his short sight and having to wear glasses. The Swan Child might grant that wish, at least, I thought.

Then we scrambled down the steep track again. I'd been a little disappointed that Uncle Christy didn't give us our sandwiches to eat on the hill itself, but once I had been up there and seen all the people, I was happy to go down and eat in his huge cool kitchen, which has a brick floor worn into ancient bumps and curves, and old black beams with hooks in them, for hanging herbs and flitches of bacon. We had our sandwiches at his long kitchen table where Mrs. Goodyear, his housekeeper, has all the French loaves and butter and cheese and pickles and salads and cold roast beef and sausages for making bar food. We offered to help her but she said, "Sit still while ye can, childer. Ye've a fair step ahead of ye still."

"We kept up an average speed of three miles an hour coming," said Jake. "We ought to be able to do about the same going back." But Uncle Christy shook his head and said we'd probably find the last four or five miles on the way back much harder going, and would be bound to find ourselves slowing down.

Going back, of course, wasn't such fun, because it was all flat country ahead, the hills were behind us; and there wasn't the excitement of unknown territory; we had seen it all before. We began to argue about the words of songs and their tunes; Jake can never carry a tune in his head, though he *thinks* he can. And after a while, fed up with one another, we walked apart, in silence, Jake about twelve yards ahead. I didn't mind; I went back to thinking about Clarissa Forbes.

They don't realize I know that, but I do, she had said. There are three of us, Esme and Ag and me. Esme is our organizer. And Ag is the servant. Originally there were four.

But how could she *not* know about them, if they all lived in the same house, and that quite a small bungalow? And who had the fourth been, the one who had gone?

At six, she had said, I change into one of the others. What could she have meant by that?

I trotted, to catch up with Jake, and said, "Do you think she was mad?"

"Who?"

"Clarissa Forbes."

"Of course," he said. "Crackers. Barmy. A screw loose. Rats in the upper story."

"Her picture wasn't mad. It was wonderful."

"How do you know? How do you know what makes a mad picture? Anyway there have been lots of mad painters. Van Gogh cut his ear off." Then he began to sing, "She was just a beautiful picture, In a beautiful golden frame," because he knew it would annoy me, so I dropped behind again.

Don't come after six, she had said. The others wouldn't like to see you at all. There might be trouble.

What sort of trouble? I wondered. It did sound queer —frightening, really. We had certainly better not call after six. And it was nearly that now—Uncle Christy had been right, our pace was growing slower and slower. But still, I thought, I would go back to the Bungalow tomorrow morning. I was dying to have another look at that picture.

When we reached the last piney hillock that lay between us and the village, our pace had dwindled to a slow, careful trudge. We weren't limping, because we had been careful to wear old thick shoes and socks, so we didn't have blisters, but our feet were tired and aching.

At this point Jake, just to show off, had to break into a run.

"I'm as chip-chip-chipper as a chipmunk, I'm as hop-hop-hoppy as a cricket!" he sang, or bawled, and went bounding over the top of the little hill. Then I heard an angry yell, a crash, and a curse. When I followed over the hill and down the slope on the other side, I found him lying in a heap at the bottom. From a big slide mark it was plain what had happened—he had slipped on the pine needles, which were smooth as glass, just about, tobogganed down the slope, tripped over a stump, and crashed into a pine tree. He had knocked himself half silly; and, what was more frightening, his leg was quite evidently broken. It stuck out sideways in a horrible way.

"Oh, Jake!"

" 'M all right," he muttered dazedly. "In half a minute —just give me a hand up—I'll be able to hop, if you find a stick—"

We tried for a yard or two, but it was hopeless; by mistake, he touched the ground with the foot of his broken leg and let out a yell of agony.

"You mustn't go any farther, it would be crazy," I said. "It might do your leg awful harm. Sit here by the side of the road and I'll run on and phone from Mrs. Williams's house. I can ask Father to come down with the car and pick us up."

Jake didn't answer for a minute. He bit his lip—he was obviously almost sick with pain. At last, grudgingly, he said "Okay."

Where he was sitting was not more than a stone's throw from the Bungalow gate, outside the bushy bamboo hedge. I thought of going in there, but the Williams house was only twenty-five yards farther on and we knew her well; actually I thought she'd probably take us home in her car.

But when I got to her house I found it all locked up, and then I remembered that she had said something in the morning about spending the weekend with her sister in Folkestone.

It was another long half mile into the main part of the village. Should I go on, or back to the Bungalow, which was close at hand?

I decided to go back. My watch said six forty-five, so I

opened the garden gate with a good deal of trepidation
and crept inside.

There was nobody in the garden; the stool and easel
had gone, so I walked as far as the trellised porch and
pulled the doorbell—a blue stone on a plaited leather
thong. The bell gave a single loud jangle, and almost
immediately the door shot open; I couldn't help starting
back nervously.

The woman who had opened the door gave me an
angry look.

"Well? What do *you* want?" she snapped. "Children
aren't allowed here."

I said, "I'm very sorry. There's been an accident. My
brother's broken his leg. Do you—is there—could I possibly use your phone?"

She was totally unlike Clarissa. Her face was made up
—very much so, with bright-red lipstick, and a lot of eye
shadow, and a thick layer of orangey pancake foundation
all over. Her hair dangled round her neck in ringlets—
very unsuitably, considering her age—and she wore a
suit, tweed, also incongruous that hot evening, stock-
ings, and high-heeled shoes. What frightened me most
was that I could see, in a way, that she *was* the same
woman—her bones were the same, and those thin, thin
wrists, one scarred. I recognized a scar on her forehead
too—and yet her face was *completely* different. And I mean
really completely. I wouldn't have recognized her if—if
—if—if I hadn't known. Her voice was different too.

"Phone, phone?" she said sharply. "And why should
you do that? Who are you?"

"I'm Cicely Freeman. My family live in the brick house
next to the post office. My brother and I have been doing
a sponsored walk to the Swan Child—"

"Swan Child? What's that? I've never heard of it. And I don't *want* to! And I don't think you *can* use our phone. I'm not keen on all and sundry pushing into my house—it's not at all convenient."

I could actually see the phone, through an open door behind her, on a table in a frilly, chintzy sitting room, so I said, "Oh, *please!* I shan't be a moment, honestly—it's just to phone my father and ask him to come and pick us up. My brother's out there by the road and he's in a lot of pain—"

As I gabbled I was gently edging into the hall.

"Where is your brother? Where?" she demanded.

I made a vague gesture—I didn't want her to go out and look at Jake. The sight of her suspicious angry painted face and those ringlets was just about the last thing he needed at that moment.

She did move aside just a little, enough to allow me past her into the chintzy room, and I made a dash to the phone, picked up the receiver, and dialed our number. But the line was dead, and I soon saw why: the cord had been cut.

"Clarissa probably did that," the woman said matter-of-factly. "Just because I don't admire her pictures she flies into these childish rages—" I gaped at her stupidly as she turned back to the door and called, in a loud voice, "Did you hear what I said, Clarissa? I know what you did —you silly girl! Just out of childish temper. It's not the least use. You might as well accept that you'll never have any talent. Tom says the same. I know you are hiding out there, it's no use pretending you can't hear." She turned back to me again and went on in a conversational tone, "She thinks I don't know she lives here too. She and Tom

—that's my husband—get up to all sorts of silly games when my back's turned."

I was looking, aghast, from the slashed phone cord to Clarissa's beautiful flower picture, which lay on the floor, sliced into about twenty strips half an inch wide. Other pictures lay about, mutilated in the same way. The woman beside me glanced down at them carelessly.

"We have one of these guillotines," she explained in an offhand manner. "I used to work in an office, you know—till I found out about Clarissa." She picked up a heavy metal board with a hinged cutting blade at one side and demonstrated how it worked, chop, chop, chop. "Very useful things," she said. By this time I was frankly backing toward the door. But she followed me into the garden, still carrying the guillotine.

"Just where did you say you had been?" she demanded.

"To—to the Swan Child," I stammered. "On Abbotsbury Hill."

She shouted, "I don't believe you! There's no such place!"

But at the same moment—or almost instantly after—I heard a detached gnatlike tiny voice in my ear, or inside my own head, that whispered, "And did you make a wish for me on the Swan Child? Did you, did you?" A bubble of terror burst in my heart, I turned to fly and tripped over the length of hose tangled across the path. I'm done for now, I thought, but the woman paused to chop a length off the hose with her guillotine.

"Tom's down there," she said conversationally. "He took a fancy to spend eighty days underground. For research. He's only been down there twenty days; he has another two months to go. That is his air pipe. *Put out your hands, child!"*

But I did not put out my hands. I beat it down the path and out of the gate, like a rat getting out of its maze. And, mercifully, just at that moment, Finch's grocery van was coming along the road. Stan Budd, the driver, had already seen Jake huddled on the dusty bank and slowed down, so I was able to race along, waving my arms, and help Stan lift Jake in, while the woman from the Bungalow stood regarding us thoughtfully over her gate, still snapping her guillotine up and down.

"You wasn't in *there*—was you?" said Stan. "Blimey! You wouldn't get me in there. Clean bonkers, *she* is. I don't take the groceries in anymore, just leave them at the gate."

My teeth were still chattering. I said, "Wh-wh-what about her husband?"

"Oh, he died. Five years ago. In the cottage hospital. But she's got some notion he's still around, and a couple of others too—"

Jake had fainted when we lifted him into the van. He lay inertly at the back among cartons of raisins and Tide. As soon as we got home, mother phoned Dr. Coswold, and he came around right away and said the break was only a simple fracture, and set it on the spot.

I haven't been into the Bungalow garden again. But sometimes when I walk past I peer cautiously over the gate. Sometimes I see the angry woman, Esme, I suppose, furiously gardening with spade or shears. Sometimes, in the evening, there is a bent, bowed person, Ag, "the servant," presumably, waving a duster from door or window. She looks very like Clarissa, but thirty years older.

I have never seen Clarissa, though, and I like to think that perhaps by bringing her wish back with me from the Swan Child's hill, I was able to set her free and help her to escape from that unhappy partnership.

I can still vividly remember her picture. I hope that, some day, I shall be able to paint one as good.

Merminster

❧❧❧❧

Zawn Head, on which the music college stood, was like a great cat's paw extending into the Atlantic. The main building, Zawn Manor, had long ago proved insufficient and had been supplemented by brick and stone annexes, and then, as students proliferated, by wooden halls, classrooms, and practice rooms, but all these were decently tucked away among the oak woods that grew almost to the cliff edge, so that the ancient stone manor house appeared much as it ever had, solitary among its roses and rhododendrons. Peaceful, it seemed, but the sounds of its present function floated from every window: voice, piano, clarinet, drum, saxophone, violin. It was held by the natives of South Cornwall that more nightingales and nighthawks frequented Zawn woods than were to be heard in any other part of the county, lured there by the musical competition from the students, who were as audible by night as they were by day. In summer every grove, tussock, rock ledge, inlet, and clump of heather on the headland was occupied by some energetically practicing soloist or group; and a glider or balloonist floating over must have been lifted upward by the sheer volume of rising sound.

Only one area remained undisturbed. This was the rose garden, which lay directly between the manor house and the head of the point. The windows of the library opened onto it, and the director's study; these were enclaves of silence. A path led from the garden down to a tiny cove, tucked so steeply between the toes of the headland that it was invisible from anywhere save the sea itself. The steep and winding track, known respectfully and affectionately as Pepin's Path, remained, by unwritten law, sacred to the director himself; no student, however gifted or privileged, was supposed to trespass there. A rail protected the path on its seaward side. Fame and failing sight had overtaken the professor by creeping and concurrent stages; as the newly knighted Sir Pepin, he had to be led by his daughter from the Queen's presence, and he was now obliged to feel his way by the rail up and down the familiar declivities of the track.

It was owing to his personal fame that the school had achieved its high standing and repute; he was a composer and musician of worldwide renown and massive achievement. It seemed amazing that he could combine academic duties with such a steady and impressive output of work, yet, year after year, the school flourished while symphonies, chamber music, operas, and oratorios continued to flow from him with apparently undiminished vigor. Blindness had neither impaired nor decreased his inspiration; if anything, music seemed to stream from him with greater power and urgency since the distractions of visual experience had been removed. He used a specially adapted Braille music typewriter for his work; and, since the administration of the college was now undertaken by his co-director, Dr. Irene Koningen, his daily tutorials and listening to the sea, which he did every afternoon, rain or fine, were his only occupations apart from composition.

"A musician *must listen,*" he told his students, over and over. "Listen to the grass, to grasshoppers, listen to moles burrowing, listen to voices, listen to traffic on the highway, listen to machinery at its work, but, above all, listen to water, listen to the sea."

So, on this warm, still foggy afternoon of late August, Sir Pepin's feet found their slow, confident way down the rock steps of the path, worn hollow like the stairway of some twelfth-century keep; and he settled himself into his accustomed place, a stone seat carved into the cliff at one of the crescent tips of his little beach. Fitting his white staff into its accustomed slot (that staff which was used, also, as a conductor's baton), he sat musing in his favorite position, knees crossed, white-bearded chin on fist, craggy blind head lifted to catch the swell and murmur of the idle sea. The tide was high, and a warm wild smell of seaweed, floating driftwood, and wet rock caused his nostrils to expand with satisfaction.

But after a moment or two he remarked in the mild yet firm tone which had imbued generations of students with instant, unquestioning, awed obedience:

"Who is there? Tell me what you are doing here, if you please."

A regretful sigh was, for a moment, his only answer.

"Who is it?" repeated Sir Pepin.

"Oh, I was so certain you wouldn't hear me if I sat perfectly still. But I might have known that I was wrong!"

The voice, no more than a reluctant murmur, had just a hint of confiding amusement in it.

"You did this for a bet, I conclude?" The severity of

the director's tone did not decrease, but the student's expression relaxed.

"Oh, good heavens, no, sir, I wouldn't dream of doing anything so vulgar."

"Then why are you here? It is Aymon Bryan, is it not?"

Sir Pepin made no favorites, remaining barricaded behind his blindness and a cloud of preoccupation with his own work; in any case, the more highly he thought of any student, the more exacting and critical he became; but still, a certain unexpressed sympathy had sprung up in this instance between teacher and disciple. Bryan addressed his principal apologetically but without too much alarm.

"Yes, sir, and I am very sorry indeed that I disturbed you. I will leave you at once."

"Wait a moment. Why did you come? If it was not for a bet—what *was* it for?"

The student hesitated for a moment. During this time the silence between them became charged with mystery and vitality.

At length Bryan answered. "Well, sir—I'm afraid you will think my reason very childish—but I had a dream about this place, this cove. I had never been down here—because of its being private—and, and I couldn't help wondering if it looked the same as it had in my dream."

He stopped. The director waited, as if expecting more remarkable revelations than this, but none came. Bryan stood with his hands clenched together; he seemed to be forcing himself to keep words locked inside him.

At last the old blind man sighed, looking suddenly no more than that: a blind, old man. Lately his friends had noticed a diminution of his usual energy; sometimes he wore a bewildered look, as if he had just woken from a deep sleep.

He asked, in a quiet, noncommittal voice, "And was it the same?"

"Yes. Yes, it was. Exactly!" Bryan's voice, quiet also, still betrayed a hint of excitement.

"Charlie's Cove, they call it." The old man smiled to himself. "Who Charlie was we don't know—do we? Was he a child picking up shells—or a shipwrecked mariner? Tell me"—now the director's voice sharpened, became fiercely inquisitorial—"tell me, do you hear any *sound,* as you stand here?"

"Sound, sir?" Now the student's tone was nervous again. "Apart from the sea, do you mean? What kind of sound?"

"Oh—for instance—the sound of bells?"

"There would have to be a west wind to bring the sound of bells from Monadnock," replied Bryan cautiously. "The wind's due south, sir."

Sir Pepin sighed. "Very well," he said coldly after a moment. "You may go, boy. Run away and get on with your work. What progress are you making with your Mass?"

"I—I have got as far as the Sanctus, sir—"

"Well, go and apply yourself to it, get back to work." Now the old man sounded both weary and impatient. "And don't come down here again without permission."

"No. And I am very sorry, sir." But still there remained that hint of excitement in the boy's voice.

Sir Pepin listened to his footsteps, climbing the rock path, and thought, What had he seen that he didn't mention?

Instead of getting on with his Mass, Bryan made his way to the college library. This, on a Saturday afternoon, was deserted. Climbing up and down ladders, Bryan pulled out book after dusty book. At last, in a fat old compendium of legends, printed in close, dark, nine-teenth-century type on crumbling yellow paper, he found what he was searching for:

After the Emperor Charlemagne had won a great victory at the battle of Saragossa, an angel came to him in a dream and ordered him to build an enormous church, which must not be founded upon land but should float abroad upon the ocean itself, so that it might carry the message of salvation to all inhabitants of the earth, from the coast of Europe to the lands of the Saracens, and as far east as Cathay. "How shall I achieve this?" objected Charlemagne. "Such a thing is impossible." "No, it is not impossible," said the angel. "You must employ the enchanter Maugis, and then it can be done." So when Charlemagne awoke, he sent for Maugis and ordered him to build such a church, even if it cost all the gold in the emperor's treasury. And Maugis set to work, using stone and brick, wood of all kinds, gold, silver, brass, marble, and copper, glass from Venetia, and precious stones from Ophir. Year by year the church rose higher, anchored in the Rhine. And Lucifer, the lord of light (and of lies), was greatly disturbed to see it growing so fast. "If that church is finished," he said to himself, "my rule over the kingdoms of Earth will be greatly diminished." So he whispered in the ear of the servant, Benedetta, who cooked for Maugis and took care of his home. This woman was a very skilled cook, and prepared, twice each day, with meats and spices and herbs, dishes fit for an emperor. But

Maugis ate them, day after day, without comment. And one evening Benedetta said to him bitterly, "My work is every bit as skilled as yours. But what comes of it? Every day you eat it up without remark, and it is gone. When I am dead, nobody will remember me, or say, 'She was the most skillful cook in seven kingdoms.' It is unjust!" But Maugis, busy with his calculations relative to the height of the twin spires, merely replied, "Peace, woman, do not trouble me with your trifling annoyances!"

After twenty years, the great cathedral was finished, and in it, on Christmas Day in the year 800, Pope Leo III crowned Charlemagne Emperor of all the Christian World. All who saw the cathedral or entered it said that no such wonder had ever existed before. But the woman Benedetta asked private audience of Charlemagne, and whispered to him secretly words of evil counsel which had been put into her head by Lucifer, the prince of wickedness. The Emperor Charlemagne, alas! possessed those faults which come with greatness. He had Maugis seized by his executioners and blinded, "In order," he said, "that he may never build another such church for any other prince who might thereby gain equal renown with that of Charlemagne." But ill came of this ill deed, for Maugis, enraged by the emperor's ingratitude, called down a curse on him. "Beautiful as the church may be," he cried in his blind grief and fury, "it shall float unseen for two thousand years, except by those who are soon to die. Deep as the spires are high, a whirlpool shall follow it through the ocean, and any ship that comes within sight of the spires shall be doomed to destruction. And as for you, cruel-hearted emperor, may you sigh for your church from age to age but never set foot in it until you have atoned, by repentance and long service, the ill that you have wrought! And may that way be set about with pitfalls and backslidings!" Groping about him in the church, Maugis found a great nine-branched glass candelabrum, which was made like a branch of cherries, with red fruit and white fruit. "I designed this to give you light, but you have left me in the dark!" he cried. "So I will take it away, and not until the last of these fruits is returned to its place shall my curse come to its end, you unjust ruler! And the first grief from it shall be yours, for your eldest son shall perish with me in the whirlpool." So saying, Maugis rushed from the cathedral. And a circular pit appeared in the waters of the Rhine and swallowed him, and after him, the emperor's son, who pursued him. Then Charlemagne grieved bitterly and repented of his deed, but it was too late; and when he returned to his capital of Aix, the cathedral broke loose from its moorings and floated down the Rhine to the sea, and it has never been seen from that day on, except by mariners, and, of those, most perished shortly after seeing it. By them it is given the name of Merminster, or the Kelpies' Kirk, or the Trolls' Temple, or the Devil's Dome.

Quietly Bryan shut the book and returned it to its place. Then, deep in thought, he wandered away to an empty practice room and, after sitting for some time plunged in reverie, he immersed himself in work on his Mass for eight voices.

He had planned a divided choir arrangement by which he hoped to achieve a contrast of great pain and grief on one side, combining with joy and hope on the other, so as to form a dialogue and, at the conclusion, a unity through which all the elements would mingle in a powerful intensity of praise and thanksgiving.

Absorbed in composition, he became wholly indifferent to the passage of time; hours passed unnoticed, until dark fell. At last, numb, stiff, drained of energy, he shuffled his manuscript pages together and walked out into the grassy quadrangle that had replaced the old manorhouse farmyard. There he encountered Hildegarde, the director's daughter, a girl of great and distinguished beauty.

"*There* you are! I thought you must have fallen into the sea," said she, laughing. "You look half stunned, as if you had been swimming for hours and hours, like a shipwrecked sailor."

"So I have! 'But I beneath a rougher sea, And whelmed in deeper gulfs than he.' "

"Well, now, come along and have some fish and chips in the village," said Hildegarde commandingly, and she tucked her arm through his and led him away from the college buildings.

As they walked along the drive, between high-massed rhododendron bushes, she asked eagerly, "Have you said anything to Father yet?"

"About our getting married? No, I haven't."

"But I thought I saw you go off down Pepin's Path after lunch?"

"So I did."

"Didn't Father come?"

"Yes, he came, but—"

"But you got cold feet at the last minute." Now her voice began to hold more than a touch of scorn.

He answered, curt with fatigue, "No. It wasn't that. Hildegarde—have you noticed anything strange about your father lately?"

"He seems rather tired—distracted—a bit absent-minded. That's just why I think we ought to tell him soon about our plans—get matters fixed up—"

"You haven't heard him speak of a cathedral—ever?"

"A cathedral? No." She seemed astonished. "What can you mean? The Wessex Choral Festival? He's anxious about that, I know—but otherwise—Look, would you prefer that I spoke to him?"

"No, no, I'll speak, I'll do it tomorrow. What is he working on himself at present, do you know?"

Hildegarde, not at all interested in her father's work, which she considered boring, old-fashioned, and pompous, said sharply that she really had no idea; then, after a moment, admitted grudgingly that it might be some choral piece, a Mass perhaps.

When they arrived at the fish-and-chip shop, "Do you want cod or plaice?" he inquired.

"Plaice. And I'll pay," she snapped. "You haven't any money."

"This represents a very considerable step forward, you know," the director told Bryan at his next tutorial, feeling his way through the manuscript, which his secretary had retyped into Braille. "I am pleased with it. In fact, it is the best thing you have done yet."

Bryan was startled. Never before had the director commended him in such direct, unqualified terms. The old man went on, "You have not completed the rest of the work—have you?"

"No, sir."

"Well. Then I tell you what I shall do. In order to give it a chance of being heard this year, I shall incorporate it in my Mass for Souls at Sea, which, as you may know, is to be performed at the Wessex Choral Festival in October."

"But, sir!"

"I am doing you a considerable favor by making use of it in this way," the director added rather impatiently. "It is nothing new, as you must be aware, for pupils' work to be incorporated in the oeuvre of a master. If you are able to finish the Agnus Dei in time, I may make use of that too. I have been overwhelmed by pressure of duties lately and am somewhat in arrears with my own composition."

It was perhaps fortunate that Sir Pepin was not able to see the expression on his pupil's face. Bryan remained silent, but it was a silence of outrage, not compliance. In a single moment, all his reverence, all his devotion, had withered away. His knees shook, with rage, not fear, as he stood up. Now he began to understand how Sir Pepin had managed to maintain his high output for so long.

"You may as well leave this with me," said the old man, laying a proprietary hand over the Braille manuscript. Then, as if as an afterthought, he remarked, "Ahem; perhaps you would be kind enough to give me your arm down to the cove. I find myself unusually tired this afternoon."

In no very solicitous frame of mind, Bryan took the

director's arm and guided his teacher through the rose garden to the cliff path. Hildegarde, watching from her bedroom window, saw the pair and gave Bryan an approving wave. His face remained impassive. True enough, he thought, this ought to be an ideal time to broach the question of our marriage. Never had he felt less inclination for the business. However, done it must be, for Hildegarde expected it, so, halfway down the silent descent, he made his request, in plain, courteous, and formal language.

After all, he thought, the old—so-and-so—is getting my Sanctus; he may consider it a reasonable exchange for his daughter.

But the old man did not.

"Marry Hildegarde? You want to marry *my daughter?*" His voice had become cold as liquid air. "What makes you think you have any right to expect such a connection?"

"We love each other," said Bryan stolidly.

"*Love?* Something more than *that* is required before I give my only child to the first comer. How do you propose to support her, may I ask?"

"We both intend to teach, sir, though of course I hope that Hildegarde will give up her job when I have established my reputation."

"And how long do you suppose *that* will take?" demanded the old man. "Come back, if you please, in four years, in six years," he added haughtily. "Hildegarde's comfort is not to depend on such a chancy thing as your reputation. Good god, no!"

Having reached the cove, he felt his way to the stone seat and sat down. "Thanks; you may leave me now. Be so good as to let Hildegarde know that she may come down and guide me back at five."

Then he turned his blind head to the sea and asked, with a faint wistfulness, "Er—just before you go—you do not see any vessel or craft out there, by any chance, do you? I thought—but I may have been deluded—that I caught the sound of a ship's bell."

Angrily Bryan turned to stare out into the golden haze; it was another still, close, misty, fragrant late-summer afternoon. There, only a bowshot's length from shore, floated the teasing mirage, the incredible creation, half concealed by drifting wreaths of sea fog, its pinnacles, gargoyles, carvings, and columns evanescent, rosy, and gilded, just as he had seen them, first in his dream, then at the same spot three days ago. The immense, unbelievable structure rocked and drifted, idling on a full tide; from it, faint, sonorous, infinitely mournful, came the sound of voices chanting, and a single bell.

"No, sir," said Bryan. His voice was cold and defiant. "There is nothing to be seen."

He picked up from the sandy beach a single crystal cherry, deep red with a freckle of gilding, and hurled it furiously out to sea.

When he had climbed halfway up the cliff he turned to look back. From there he could still see the old man sitting forlornly, chin on fist, staring into vacancy. Beyond were the twin spires, and beyond them, deep and deadly as Charybdis, a great whirling funnel in the sea.

In the sea, thought Bryan, or in his mind? Angrily he turned and hurried on.

Mrs. Chatterbox

❦❦❦

Neil had slept badly at High Hardland, the farm where they had stayed last night. Roosters! Lord, how they did keep crowing! *Cock-a-doodle-doo, cock-a-doodle-doo,* one after another, shouting their heads off, across what sounded like immense distances, from one side of the place to the other. It was a mournful sound, as if they asked some question without an answer, or hopelessly waited for somebody to contradict them. Well, that was the disadvantage of putting up at farms, he supposed; you had to accept the roosters, and the melancholy *baa*-ing of the sheep, the cattle sounding off at regular intervals all night, like foghorns. But Helen had been set on the notion of staying at farms, and he was bound to say they had found some really nice places. Helen had brought the Tourist Board list of farm accommodations along, and they had phoned ahead each day, picking a place that looked just beyond their hiking distance—"So as to give us a challenge," Helen had said—and then battling to get there before dark. No problem, mostly, about getting in at this time of year; it was mid-October, and most of the places that took summer guests had plenty of rooms; some indeed had closed down for the winter, but they could generally suggest another place within the same range: "Juist a brither and sister, for the one nicht, is it? Mrs. Gowrie, beyont the post office, she'll have ye, and glad to; it's the wee white hoose wi' the twi windies either side o' the door."

And certainly last night's had been a pleasant enough place: High Hardland, it deserved its name, on the very peak of a moor, with a handful of ragged trees leaning around it as if for protection, and friendly people; but the bed had been lumpy, or damp, or something, and the cocks kept waking Neil, and in between he had frightful dreams about this old woman with a three-syllable name, who kept running after him and begging him to remember her.

"Ye'll no forget puir auld Elspeth Moneybox?" Stretching out skinny beseeching arms after him, then putting herself in front, scurrying ahead, so that in his haste to get away he nearly tripped over her. She smelled truly terrible, and her clothes were all in tatters, and she kept rattling on, in a way that he could hardly understand.

"I can't make head or tail of what you're *saying!*" he wanted to shout. "It's *my* dream, you silly old fool. You ought to speak so that I know what you're going on about —if you *must* speak."

"Och, laddie, ye've a kind face, a kind kenspeckit face. Ye'll put right the wrong that was done to puir auld Elspeth Moneybox?"

"That's an *idiotic* name, you can't possibly be called Elspeth Moneybox!"

But still she kept jabbering after him, her words clacking out of her like the rattle of castanets. And when he woke up, trying to get away from her, *cock-a-doodle-doo!*

cock-a-doodle-doo! in the pitch-dark, long, long before dawn; and each time, when he drifted back into sleep again, there the old hag was waiting for him: "Ye'll no forget puir auld Elspeth Buttonbox?"

It was a huge relief to come down, heavy-eyed, to breakfast by the fire in the cozy farm parlor, thick porridge, homemade bread and butter, eggs and great slabs of bacon, tea so strong that it practically sang inside your head. But, later in the day, that breakfast had sat heavily in his stomach, and now his head ached and ached; for the last two or three hours' walking he had been silent and surly, hardly bothered to answer Helen's remarks.

They were walking through a pass between two mountains, Ben More and Ben Lairg.

"They ought to be called Ben More and Ben Less," Helen had suggested, and he had treated that with the silence it deserved. The track was marked, here and there, with white-painted posts or stones, and this was just as well, for although from a distance the pass looked strikingly unmistakable, a tremendous V, splitting the range of hills like an axe cleft, when you actually got up there, you found a confusing complexity of tracks running off hither and thither, up the hillside and down into gullies. And, high up here, there was a thin mist, or haar, as they had learned to call it, which reduced visibility to about twenty yards around them. It was silent too; apart from the occasional caw of a crow or whicker of a grouse, not a sound to be heard.

Neil walked a few yards ahead. Occasionally glancing back out of the corner of his eye he could see that Helen was limping slightly, doing her best to conceal the fact. Earlier she had asked if he had any moleskin left, and he said no, he'd used his last piece. She should have bought more when they were in Colliemuir; the way they'd come, across country, there just weren't any houses or shops. She ought to have brought some with her, silly girl! Anyway, today was the last, tomorrow they'd get the night train from Rosstown back to London. Tonight's lodging was still in question, though; they simply hadn't passed through a single place all day from which they could telephone. On the map a little hamlet called Glenhulish looked as if it might offer houses, a callbox, maybe a shop; but when they got there they found it was deserted, derelict, just a few crumbling walls, a couple of chimney stacks poking up among nettles, tansy, teazel.

"We must be nearly through the pass," Helen remarked presently. She had the map. "Look, that high peak ahead must be Ben Athill, which is on the other side of the Garple Valley." The mist had shifted slightly—or perhaps it was because they had descended, coming out of the hills; they could see a wide, deep valley opening at right angles to their course. The track slanted down into it, taking a leftward turn, with pine forest on the right below and rocky heathery hillside above on the left.

"And, see, here's a likely-looking place called Killiemuir Farm," Helen went on, stabbing at the map with her finger. "It's down by the Garple and looks quite big. I expect we could get a bed for the night there, or they could tell us where else to try. It's only about an hour's walk from here."

"Well, I just hope they *can* have us," Neil said dourly. "I don't know about you, but I'm bushed."

He hated admitting it; Helen was two years younger. But lately she had grown a lot, and was now taller by an inch. When they had been younger, and he the bigger of the two, Neil used to tease her quite a bit, tweaking her hair, putting her in armlocks, and holding her head under the blankets, things like that; but for the last couple of years he had more or less given up these practices, fearing that she might be able to give as good as she got.

On the whole they got on comfortably enough.

This walking trip had been Helen's idea. She had planned the whole thing, bought the maps, and sent away for the list of farms, and he was bound to say it had worked out quite well. Until today. If only he didn't feel so gray and heavy—not ill, exactly, just unutterably low and depressed. That dismal dream kept rattling back and forth inside his head, aggravating his weary exasperation, as if some creature inside his skull were begging to be let out.

"Ye'll no forget puir auld Elspeth Windowbox? Ye'll mind puir Elspeth Chickenpox? Remember Elspeth Alpenstocks! Ah, ye'll mind puir wee Elspeth Goldilocks?"

"Oh, shut up, will you!" he snapped, and realized that he had spoken aloud in a vain effort to still the clatter inside his head.

"I only asked the time," said Helen, injured.

"Sorry. I was thinking." He grunted. "It's five past three. Look, I can see smoke ahead, above those trees."

The track ran steeply down to a main road, the first they had seen that day. They followed it for a quarter of a mile, then came to a road sign indicating a left turn ahead.

"That must be Killiemuir Farm," said Helen, relieved. Her limp had become more pronounced on the hard road.

But when they reached the turn-off they were dismayed to see a new painted sign by it: KILLIEMUIR FARM HOTEL   *Licensed Accommodation.*

"Oh, gosh! How awful!" Helen came to a stop. "Someone must have taken it over and turned it into a hotel. Now what'll we do?"

"We certainly can't afford to stay at a hotel," Neil said sourly. They had only a few pounds left and their train tickets back to London. He scowled at Helen as if she were to blame, though realizing that this was unfair. "Let's look at the map again; maybe there's something else."

But the map told them, unequivocally, that there was no other habitation for at least six miles.

"I'm going to go down and ask," said Helen at length. "Perhaps they'll have a barn or trailer where they'll let us sleep; or maybe they'd give us a bed in exchange for peeling potatoes or washing dishes."

She began limping down the track.

"Washing *dishes*," sneered Neil, reluctantly going after her. "Are you crazy? They're hardly likely to have so many guests now that they'd want dishwashers."

His spirits felt even lower than they had up among the mountains. There was something unutterably dismal about this track running down and down between close-set evergreens, larch or firs, which presently gave way to banks of high, dark rhododendrons. Then suddenly they came out on to a newly graveled flat space in front of Killiemuir Farm.

"Oh, lord, it's big," said Neil, and, "Help!" exclaimed Helen simultaneously in dismay, "they've got *masses* of guests!"

"All the more need for extra dishwash hands," pointed out Neil dryly. "Okay, *you* go and ask, as it was your idea. I'll just wait here." He had noticed a stone bench under an ilex tree at the side of the graveled parking area; he walked across and plumped himself down on it.

Helen gave him a hunted look, but said, after a moment, "Oh, all right. I'll go to the back door, I think."

She vanished around the side of the house, which seemed, Neil thought, halfway between a farm and a manor. Behind, on a lower level going down toward the river, could be seen barns, sheds, haystacks, and the house itself, a rambling affair, stone-built and slate-roofed, unpretentious; but at some point, perhaps in the early nineteenth century, a grand front had been stuck onto it, with two high crow-stepped gables, castellations like a lower row of false teeth across the top, and a round, pepper-pot turret at each corner, beginning halfway up.

The effect was quite handsome in a way, like a sort of junior castle, thought Neil dispassionately; but just the same he didn't like the place. Hated it, in fact. He hoped that Helen's mission would prove fruitless, even if it meant another six-mile hike along the hard main road.

But here was Helen coming back, beaming like a Cheshire cat.

"It's all right! They're really pleased to have us! I'm going to help wash dishes—one of the kitchen staff is sick, and they're expecting a big batch of guests for the shooting. And you're to paint a room. Mr. Jardine—that's their name, they're awfully nice—he was doing it, but now he has to do the cooking. So come on—he says it won't take long—"

She was dragging Neil toward the back door, across a cobbled farmyard.

"Paint a room?"

"Yes, it's half done. This is my brother, Mrs. Jardine. He's quite used to house-painting, he does lots of it at home—"

Mrs. Jardine, short, sturdy, and yellow-haired, would have been quite nice-looking if she hadn't been so red and shiny in the face. She gave Neil a beaming but distracted smile.

The kitchen, he saw, had recently been modernized, probably several little sculleries and pantries thrown into one; it was dazzling-clean and lavishly equipped, several big stoves and refrigerators, rows of catering-size pans on the wall; and delicious smells wafted from the ovens. A thin, harassed man in a chef's apron also gave Neil a friendly but preoccupied grin.

"Hallo there, you going to help us out? You couldn't have arrived at a better moment. My wife'll show you what wants doing."

Mrs. Jardine, without more ado, led them through a big square hall with antlers on the walls and stuffed fish in glass cases, up a thickly carpeted flight of stairs. There was a smell of new carpet and fresh paint. Upstairs, the walls had evidently just been papered; everything was glossy and unmarked.

"It's been such a rush," explained Mrs. Jardine. "We've only been in the house two months. Hoped to get started earlier in the summer, but you know what lawyers are. . . . Now, you'll be sleeping up on the attic floor, I'll just show you where to put your things."

On up another flight, bare narrow stairs this time, and she led them to a couple of little attic bedrooms, side by side, unfurnished except for camp beds, with a view from their windows down over the cobbled farmyard and across the surging, rocky Garple River. You could hear the sound of it quite clearly from here, a kind of sighing roar.

"Oh, how wonderful!" said Helen. "These are the best rooms we've had yet, aren't they, Neil? Aren't we lucky?"

He did not say how very far from lucky he felt, how he loathed this whole house, what utter revulsion he felt at the prospect of painting one of its rooms.

"Now, here's a bathroom you can use," said Mrs. Jardine. "One thing the house *wasn't* short of." And she laughed, unaccountably, leading them down to the main floor again. "And, see, here's the room that's being painted. We haven't used this one yet but it's going to be needed this week."

She glanced at Neil doubtfully.

"It seems awful to set you to work right after you've done a long hike, but we do desperately need it finished. See, Dick's done half already—"

It was a spacious, handsome room, evidently at the front corner of the house, for two windows looked on to a neglected garden at the side and three on to the graveled parking area. The rear wall and the inner one had been painted white already; a roll of new carpet and some furniture was piled in this area. The rest of the room was bare. A ladder stood by the three front windows, with pots of paint, brushes, a roller and pan, and a canvas bag of tools.

"I'm afraid it's all the fiddly bits you have to do," said Mrs. Jardine. "I loathe painting around windows myself. Now, have you everything you need?"

Neil looked at the equipment and said yes. His tone was glum. He could feel Helen staring at him anxiously and this irritated him even more.

Mrs. Jardine said, "I expect you're both very hungry. We start serving dinner at six. Why don't you paint for a bit and then come down and have a meal with the first serving. At least we can feed you like fighting cocks in exchange for working you to death! Now you," she said to Helen, "come with me, I've got dozens of jobs for you," and she hurried away.

"Are you all right?" said Helen softly, anxiously, to Neil, who merely nodded in reply, going over to stir a pot of paint that had a mixing stick in it. A perfectly decent brand; at least the job shouldn't be a difficult one. He did not dislike painting, as a matter of fact, if only it weren't in this awful place. And white, at least, was a no-problem color; he supposed they'd picked it for the sake of light, as this seemed a dark room, a dark house, looking northward, as it did, up the thickly wooded slope of the hill.

After another doubtful glance at him, Helen followed Mrs. Jardine.

Neil did the ceiling first, because that was always the worst part, up on the ladder with your neck cricked back, paint showering on your face and running up your sleeve.

(And the awful old woman crawling about on the floor behind his ladder, muttering to herself and moaning to him: "Please dinna forget auld Elspeth Equinox. Oh, please, please remember auld Elspeth Moneybox, who niver, niver did ye the least bit o' harm. . . ." Several times he almost kicked backward, imagining her bony face at the foot of the ladder, her hands clutching for his ankles, skinny hands that were spotted all over with freckles, yellow and wrinkled as chickens' claws. . . .)

He was a bit dizzy. It was a relief to come down off the ladder and work at ground level on the front wall with the three big sash windows in it. Not a large area of wall here—he had done the worst of the job by now—but, as Mrs. Jardine had said, painting around windows was a tiresome, fiddling business, took much longer than a plain flat stretch.

("Please dinna forget auld Elspeth Paradox. Sure and ye'll mind auld Elspeth Chickenpox.")

"Shut up, you ghastly old misery!" he shouted, and then, at a gasp behind him, turned, disconcerted, to see Helen standing in the doorway.

"Neil? Was that you shouting?"

She looked very startled.

He grunted. "Nearly lost my balance. Thought I was going to fall out of the window."

All the windows were wide open, letting in sharply cold air; despite that, it was stuffy, horribly so, in the big room.

"I've come to tell you supper's ready," said Helen. "We're to eat in grandeur in the dining room; Mrs. Jardine says that's easier than having us underfoot in the kitchen."

"I must wash first, half a minute," said Neil. "And there's something I want to have a look at."

He ran along the wide passage that bisected the first floor. Doors of bedrooms opened on to it. The door at the far end stood open, and he went into the room. Helen followed him, rather nervous. "Do watch it, this may be occupied; yes, look, there are suitcases, and brushes on the dressing table."

"If they come, tell them you're turning down the beds," said Neil. "Yes, that's what I wanted to see—look, there's a john in the turret."

Since the room was at the end of the house, it had the circular turret on its outer corner; three steps approached a door opening into a small round bathroom, with a mahogany Victorian toilet seat and a tiny ancient handbasin.

"How neat!" said Helen, impressed. "That must have been done ages ago."

"Yeah, but what's odd is that the room I'm painting ought to have one too. And it doesn't. But the steps are there. Come back and I'll show you."

"There's no time. I've lots of jobs waiting. I'll come later on."

They sat for their meal at a tiny table for two close by

the kitchen door. The big dining room had also plainly been made from a couple of rooms thrown together; part of it, the far end, was still unfurnished, with a bare, newly sanded and polished floor. At the kitchen end it was carpeted, and a dozen tables were set with starched linen, plates, glasses, and flowers. A number of guests were already at supper, laughing and talking about the day's shooting. Mrs. Jardine and a flaxen-headed girl dashed to and fro with plates of food.

Passing them, Mrs. Jardine said, "Ah, you fetched your brother, that's right. How's it going?"

"About half done," said Neil, who could hardly hear her for the buzzing in his ears.

"Good boy! I daresay you're ready to eat a hippopotamus. Here's some soup to start."

He did feel hungry, but also extremely sick and faint. The soup looked good, though: thick chicken and leek. Glancing up, he was vaguely puzzled to see that the girl who put it in front of him was a skeleton: the strings of her white starched apron encircled nothing but bones.

"Is this supposed to be fancy dress, or something?" he muttered to Helen. "What's the big idea? Are they giving a Hallowe'en party?"

"Not that I know of. What are you talking about?" Helen did not seem to have observed anything out of the ordinary. She was calmly eating her soup, telling him about the Jardines.

"They only inherited this place last year. It belonged to her great-uncle—an old man who lived to ninety-five. I suppose he was the laird. His name was Mr. MacLeod, and he was so stingy that he let the whole place go to rack and ruin, never repaired anything. The farm buildings were falling down, and he'd bricked up half the windows and nailed up half the doors, to stop the cold getting in.

He used candles and lamps, wouldn't have electricity in the place. . . ."

"Enjoyed your soup? That's right. Now here's a lamb chop."

The skeleton was by them attentively again, with plates containing lamb chops, roast potatoes, and peas. Neil nearly dropped his plate. Helen took hers without the least sign of surprise and went right on with what she was saying:

"The old man lived all alone for the last twenty years. The furniture was half rotten. Mrs. Jardine said lots of it had to be burned. He didn't have any children of his own, that's why she inherited the house. . . ."

A piano stood in the dining room. Now one of the guests, who had finished his meal, began playing a Strauss waltz, and some of the others began dancing at the uncarpeted end of the room, while the rest watched, laughing and clapping their hands. A skeleton twirled imperturbably among the couples and turned, at every third beat, its grinning face in Neil's direction.

"The old man's wife had run away from him years before he died, because he was so mean, he was such a miser. . . ."

"Ready for apple tart?" politely inquired a skeleton, leaning over Helen's shoulder.

"I don't want any dessert." Neil stumbled to his feet. "I'm going to go upstairs and finish that job."

"No apple tart? But it's your favorite!" Helen looked up at him, troubled. "Are you sure you're all right? You've gone awfully pale."

"I'm okay—I'm okay. It's just that it's so stuffy in here."

Through the kitchen door he noticed the skeleton stirring something in a pan. He couldn't wait to get away from the dining room and away from Helen. By now he felt a real rage against her. *She* had brought him into this awful place. He'd have liked to kick her shins, pull her hair, twist her arms behind her back. Once, when she was much smaller, he had shut her in a closet and left her there, screaming and screaming, for an hour and a half; they were alone together in the house. He'd like to do that now, just to keep her quiet! Only there were no closets in those attics. But there were wardrobes in the bedrooms on the main floor. . . .

Occupied in these thoughts, he returned to work. It was dark by now, much harder to see if he was making a proper job of it. Really one shouldn't paint by artificial light. Still, if the Jardines were in such a hurry . . .

He painted the side wall with the two windows; that didn't take long. Now there only remained the corner: three steps up and a flat area of diagonal wall, about twice the size of a door. Quite plainly there *must* have been a door here once, leading into another turret room like that at the other end.

He tapped with the handle of his brush. The sound was hollow. When he slapped on a brushful of wet paint the surface began to wrinkle.

Paper. No use painting on that. It would only come away, peel off when it was covered with paint.

There was a stripping spatula among the tools in the canvas bag; he began scraping off the damp paper, which came away in long peeling curls. Beneath it he discovered a mahogany door matching the one in the other end room.

("Och, puir wee Helen! Ye'd not be so unkind as to shut her up? Not like puir auld Elspeth Goldenlocks? Ye'd not be so ill-natured as that?" The awful old woman was back; more imploring, more insistent than ever. He kept thinking he could feel clawlike hands snatching at his ankles.)

There was a bitter draft coming from under the mahogany door. Why hadn't somebody done something about that long ago? But no doubt the Jardines had had their hands full, trying to get the place habitable in only two months.

"Oh, gosh, Neil!" That was Helen's voice. She had said something about bringing him up some coffee. Now here she was holding a mug. She looked horrified at the uncovered mahogany door. "I don't think you ought to have done that—"

Suddenly wild with rage, he flung down the knife, rushed at her, thrust her out of the room and into the bedroom next door, where there was a huge, old-fashioned wardrobe—shoved her inside and locked the door, despite her screams and shouts. "Neil, have you gone *crazy*? What's come *over* you? Let me out! Let me out of here at once! *Neil!*"

Ignoring her cries, he hurried back to his job.

Almost all the paper was off now; only a few scraps remained. Soaking and rubbing, he soon had them peeled away. There was a half-inch gap under the door, which the paper had partly masked; no wonder he had felt such a draft! Now it was plain that the door had been fastened shut with five large nails, ruthlessly hammered into the dark-brown polished mahogany. What a way to treat a good piece of wood! And why nail it shut, why not lock it? Why paper over it?

Then he recalled Helen's voice, which he had hardly heeded at the time, saying, "The old man was so stingy that he shut up all the bathrooms in the house, to avoid paying rates on them. . . ."

The nails, rusty with damp, resisted his efforts to pull

them out, but with pliers and hammer-claw he presently had four of them lying on the steps. Only one left. Soon he would have it out too. . . .

Vaguely, as he pulled and dragged, he became aware that another person had entered the room behind him and let out some exclamation. But now, suddenly, the door flew open, and out of it, on to him, lurched the thing that had been leaning against it: a heavy, mummified body, dressed in crumbling, rotten rags, the grinning glare of its fleshless face appearing to greet Neil as, collapsing against him, it seemed to embrace him with its thin arms.

He reeled backward down the steps, falling into a black well of terror, through which the thing pursued him, clumping on its naked heel bones, clattering its yellow teeth, calling, "Wait, wait, wait for me, wait for Elspeth Pillarbox!"

"Keep away!" he screamed. "You keep away from me, you hateful old hag!"

At last, in mercy, some concerned person thrust a needle into his arm and pressed home the plunger. The rattle of bones diminished; his frenzied dream leveled off into the calm black of unconsciousness.

When next he woke, it was daylight; he could hear no sound except, in the distance, the soft roar of the river. He lay totally limp, exhausted, sick, but at peace, knowing that he was free again, he was his own master. The frightfulness that had pursued him all yesterday had at last relaxed its grip. His head no longer ached. The nagging voice had died away.

But then a different horror seized him. Helen! He had locked her up in a wardrobe! How could he have been mad enough to do such a thing?

He let out some inarticulate cry, and, almost immediately, Helen herself was in the room. She looked white and alarmed.

"Neil! Are you all right? Heavens, what an awful thing to happen!"

"Wh—what did happen?" he croaked, finding his voice with difficulty.

"Why—you found that body—the body that had been shut up in the turret!"

Now Mrs. Jardine hurried in and carefully felt his forehead.

"No fever, thank the lord! Och, my, we've been worried to death about you. Poor boy. Poor boy!"

"Then it was *real?* That? But didn't I shut you in a wardrobe?" he said to Helen.

"No. Why should you think so? I was working down in the kitchen all evening. Mr. Jardine brought you up some coffee—to see how you were getting on—then we heard him let out *such* a shout—"

"Who was it?" Neil asked. "The—the person in the turret?"

"Why," said Mrs. Jardine, after a pause, "the police reckon it must have been old Mrs. MacLeod. She hadn't been seen for twenty years before the old man died. Everyone thought she had run away from the old tyrant. Poor great-aunt Elspie—I can remember my mother talking about her. When she was young she was a silly, cheerful body—you couldn't imagine a more ill-matched pair, Mother used to say. She'd rattle on and rattle on, and the old man used to fly into a rage with her, and shout, 'Hold yer whisht, ye daft old chatterbox, or one o' these days I'll shut ye up for good and all. . . .' "

Two Races

～～～

The year was 1930, and the month was April; it had been a bitterly cold, wild, gale-racked season, and the Brittany moors were still patched with snow as Inspector Vidame's train made its leisurely way toward the coast, stopping at ever smaller places along the way. At last, looking out, he saw the sign ZINZAC-MONT and prepared to alight. His final destination was Zinzac-Plage, but the railway did not go that far.

"Can I get a taxi?" he asked the stationmaster, but the man shook his head.

"The road is too bad, monsieur. We had a severe frost last night. No driver will risk it until the ice has melted on the hill. You will have to take the cliff railway."

"Direct me to it."

The stationmaster merely pointed. Beyond the station building lay a wide cobbled square with a few pointed, high-gabled buildings dotted around its perimeter, screened from each other by large trees. Directly across the square from the station a tiny gothic building enclosed by spiky iron railings bore the sign CLIFF RAILWAY.

(first appeared in Isaac Asimov magazine)

Inspector Vidame walked over to it, shivering in the icy breeze, which felt and smelled as if it had traversed miles of snow-covered empty land. Brittany was a queer, primitive, cut-off place, he thought; the people looked different, not French; they had their roots back in a wilder, darker pre-Christian era.

Passing through the iron gates, he found a grim old lady at a ticket booth, paid the small fare she indicated, and asked where he should go. Like the stationmaster, she merely pointed, and he saw that he must step into a small, cabinlike waiting room.

Taciturn lot, thought the inspector. No wonder the local police made so little progress in the case.

Entering the cabin, he realized that he was, in fact, entering the rail car itself: a glass-enclosed structure, perhaps eight feet square, equipped with wooden benches; below it, for its base, was a triangular tank, which was slowly filling with water from a conduit at the rear.

Looking out of the front window, Inspector Vidame was presented with a panoramic view of Zinzac-Plage three hundred feet below him at the foot of the cliff. The tiny port clustered on either side of a rocky torrent that rushed into the Atlantic, dividing around an island just large enough to contain three houses. This was connected by bridges to the riverbanks on either side. A large stone wall enclosed a small harbor. Beyond it extended a snow-encrusted stretch of beach, and there were some of the trappings of a holiday resort—a bandstand, ornamental gardens, and wrought-iron benches. A few snow-laden palms shivered miserably in the wind.

Creeping up what seemed an almost vertical incline below him was the other cable car, and as Vidame noticed this, his own car began to move down. The system

was primitive but effective—the bucket principle: as the
tank of one car filled at the top, its weight made it start
down, thereby hauling up the other car, which had emp-
tied its tank at the bottom. There was a general air of
damp, mold, moss, and running water about the contriv-
ance. I do hope the cables are kept well oiled, thought
the inspector; but the cliff railway had been running
since 1890, a plaque at the top told him, so presumably
the authorities in charge knew how to maintain it prop-
erly.

Halfway down, one car passed the other; the ride was
slow, and as the cars were unheated and freezing cold,
the inspector, the sole passenger, was relieved to step
out at the bottom and thread his way through the narrow
slushy streets of the lower town. Here he inquired his
way to the house of Madame Dodman and was interested
to note that the name evoked black looks. One man spat,
a woman crossed herself, and two others would not
speak but hastily went on their way.

The house he was looking for proved to be one of the
three on the central islet. The inspector crossed a bridge
over the river, which, fed by last night's snow, was hurl-
ing itself furiously toward the harbor, among boulders
big as grand pianos. The air down there was dank and
chill. From its north-facing aspect, Inspector Vidame
guessed that Zinzac-Plage, huddled at the foot of the
steep cliff, must lose the sun entirely for a proportion of
the winter; no wonder its inhabitants seemed so surly
and dour. What a place to live in! Nothing but rock,
water, and overlush vegetation, which at the moment
seemed half dead, nipped by the untimely cold.

The inspector soon realized that he would learn nothing useful from Madame Dodman. She was a slack-faced,
pale-eyed woman with wispy hair and a dirty apron. She

ran a kind of guest house, but it was hard to imagine that anybody would wish to stay there, except, perhaps, in high summer, when its location on the island might have some appeal. Now, damp, bleak, and scantily furnished, it appeared wholly unattractive, like its owner. In fact, Inspector Vidame soon decided that the poor woman must be slightly feebleminded, so haltingly and irrelevantly did she answer his questions. How could she ever manage to run a guest house? She seemed hardly capable of following a train of thought.

"It was your son who . . . vanished, madame?"

"Ah yes, ah yes . . . poor boy. . . ."

"How old was he?"

"Eh?"

"How old?"

"Fifteen. But he was not one of the . . . He never had been . . . He had no . . . Of course boys never do . . . It is girls who . . . Ah, here is my daughter."

At this moment, as if summoned by some plea in the woman's voice, a girl came into the dismal room where they were talking. It was the dining room of the guest house; four small oilcloth-covered tables and a number of spindly chairs gave a gloomy indication of the kind of food that one might expect to be served there. But the girl was in startling contrast both to the place and her mother. Tall and shapely, she moved with a smooth, fluid economy, so that although her actions did not appear to be fast, she seemed to travel from one point to another with great precision and rapidity. Her face was a pale, regular oval, and her hair was quite straight and dressed in a chignon, so black and smooth that it had blue lights in it. Her eyes seemed to be very large, but it was not possible to discover their color, for she wore tinted sunglasses, bluish and slightly opalescent, which reflected the light. They struck a note of incongruity.

"Monsieur? How can I serve you?" Her voice was level and quiet, smooth too, like everything about her.

"Daniella," said the mother helplessly, "he wants us to tell him . . . But what is there to tell?"

"They sent his hand. Wrapped in seaweed."

"His *hand?*" The inspector was appalled, but he tried to maintain an atmosphere of calm and reason. "Then perhaps—perhaps he is still alive? It is a threat, a kidnapping?"

But the mother shook her head. "No. A boy . . . a boy is of no value. . . ."

"It was a threat," said the girl. "But he is dead. I know."

"Why? And who are *they?*"

"The Herons."

Following the direction of the girl's gaze, Inspector Vidame glanced out of the window, across the sodden little patch of snowy garden and the turbulent river. On the opposite shore, in the cobbled area by the bandstand, seven or eight men were standing. They did not wave or gesticulate. They merely stood, idle and disengaged. They did not seem to look toward the house, but nevertheless there was a decided air of menace about them. They wore gray overalls. They are only sailors, surely, waiting for the tide to turn, thought the inspector. Yet they made him uneasy.

"There has always been a war between the Herons and the Colimaçons," said the girl. "Oh, it goes back . . . beyond the history books. In the caves there are pictures of their battles."

The mother began to cry, twisting her soiled apron.

"But *he* was not one! Oh, why did poor Jacques . . . ? He was neither one thing nor the other."

In some remote corner of his brain, the girl's name had been fidgeting Inspector Vidame. It sounded familiar. Now he made the connection.

"Daniella Dodman. *La Daniella*. Did you not—forgive me—can it have been some relation—your grandmother, perhaps—who was a great cabaret *artiste?*"

"Yes, it was my grandmother," said the girl tonelessly.

"She performed in Paris before the Great War? Twenty, thirty years ago?"

"She was my grandmother," the girl repeated.

And what had there been about La Daniella? Something special, something remarkable. Slowly the details came back into Vidame's mind. Her act in itself was nothing out of the ordinary, but—yes, that was it—she always wore glasses, tinted glasses, all the time she was dancing. Or a black mask. And then—if you stayed very late, and paid an extra five hundred francs—what was it that she did? Vidame had read about it. He was fascinated by such stories. There was supposed to be some kind of risk attached—a curse—like those Japanese fish that are such a popular delicacy among the sophisticates of Tokyo. One in a hundred is deadly poison; if you eat it, you writhe in agony for three days, then die. But the other ninety-nine are so delicious that some people consider them worth the risk of dying. But what was it that La Daniella had done?

"Dodman?" he said. "That is not a Breton name, surely?"

"No, there was an English ancestor, from Cornwall. Though, of course," the girl said, "there has always been a connection between Cornwall and Brittany. The races are connected."

"So the name Dodman—"

"My grandmother never married," the girl said coldly.

Nor did your mother, thought the inspector, turning to look at Madame Dodman, *Madame* by courtesy, presumably, who had begun fretfully wiping the tabletops with a damp rag. Why she bothered he could not imagine; it did not seem in the least probable that any tourists would come seeking lunches in such wintry weather, especially if the only access road to Zinzac was impassable with ice.

Wondering for the first time where the road was located, he looked out of the window again, over the open space where the gray-overalled youths loitered, above the roofs of the town, at the beetling hillside. Yes, there it ran, lacing back and forth over the snow-streaked rock— eight hairpin bends, one above the other, a marvel of road engineering. How had they managed to get into this place before the road was built? wondered the inspector. Perhaps there was another way around the coast, to Plouot-les-Pins.

The girl had followed the direction of his gaze to the road.

"On Easter night and at midsummer, they have a race," she said.

"The people here in Zinzac?"

"No. Only the Herons. Down the hill. On their motorbikes. Down, up, and down again. It is a race against the cablecar."

The skin on his head crept at the thought of taking those bends, crazily fast, on a motorbike, and at night. How many were killed every year?

"But surely," he said, "when there is ice on the hill, they cannot . . . ?"

"Ah, it was warm at Easter. That was before the snow

came. They had been tarring the road. They do that every spring—"

By *they* he gathered she meant the town authorities, not the mysterious group she called the Herons.

"And it was at Easter your brother disappeared?"

"On Easter morning he was gone. And the next day there was a sack on the doorstep with his hand in the seaweed."

"Could it be possible that he had taken part in the race? And had been killed—?"

"Oh, no. They would never allow an outsider. No, that is not how he died."

"But, mademoiselle . . ." The inspector began to feel irritated. This girl seemed so positive about the whole thing, as if she saw no reason for the law to come meddling.

Well, he supposed, from her point of view, the law could do little.

"But don't you want them punished?" he demanded.

"Oh, they will be punished," she said.

The mother looked out of the window to where a thrush was cracking a snail shell on the edge of the concrete path—*thwack, crack! Thwack, crack*—and then methodically pecking out the contents.

"Nature is so cruel . . ." said Madame Dodman dreamily. "Big, small. The big always wins. The small always loses. But then one day there will come one bigger still. It is fair. In the end, a balance is kept. Some cat will eat the thrush."

It was the longest and most rational statement Vidame had heard her make.

"But, mademoiselle, you do think that your brother has been killed?"

"I am certain of it."

"Why? What was the reason?"

The mother began to moan softly. "Oh, why did we ever come here? We should have stayed in Brest."

"Wherever you stay," said the girl, "they catch you in the end. If you have something they want, they come after you. Like the thrush."

But what is it that you have? the inspector wondered.

"Madame, mademoiselle," he said formally, "I have troubled you long enough. Will you be so kind as to direct me to the office of your local agent of police, Monsieur Thénard?"

"I will show you the way," said Daniella, picking up a basket. "I have to go out."

He reflected that she might be glad of his escort past the group of youths.

These, however, made no move or hostile gesture. Indeed, they remained unnaturally still, their attention trained entirely on the girl as she walked past them with dignity. When they were almost out of earshot, a voice chanted softly, derisively, yearningly, "Show us, show us, show us, Mademoiselle Colimaçon!"

Daniella took no notice of the voice except that her back straightened, her chin lifted, she looked rigidly ahead through her blue-tinted glasses.

"What do they want of you, mademoiselle?" asked Vidame. "What are they after?"

"You know what my grandmother did? You had heard about her performance? That is what they wish me to do for them."

Her voice was so cold and grim that the inspector shivered. If only he could recall the precise nature of La Daniella's act!

"But you will not?" he suggested.

"Do you think I would?" she said proudly. "They are

the enemy! Unless—" She stopped, bit her lip, then added, "And—after what they did to Jacques?"

"Why do they wish it so much? And what did they do to Jacques?"

"I will show you." She laid a hand on his wrist. "Look at the hill." He started at her touch, which was colder than the wet stone underfoot, then obediently raised his eyes to the hill facing them. From there they had a good view of the fantastic corniche that jagged down the cliff face like a blade of lightning. He noticed that roadmen were at work on it, sanding the surface. Even so, I would go ten miles around, he thought, rather than negotiate those bends.

"First, they cut off his hand," said Daniella. "Now look." Under the touch of her cold fingers, it seemed, the view darkened to a grayness between moonlight and dawn. Below, the town slept. Up above on the hill, dark figures were busy with ropes, not sanding the surface now but doing something else to it. Nailing, hammering. Then he heard the rising snarl of motorbike engines, the roar of acceleration. Six, seven, eight, nine, they shot down the diagonal slopes, the prongs of their headlights, like snails' eyes, crossing and recrossing on the hillside. Down they went, then turned and soared back up the hill, then down again, one after another, then up, then down, over and over.

Vidame shook himself dazedly. She let go of his wrist, and the daylight rushed back. He drew it in like air, with gratitude and terror.

"They flattened him," said Daniella. "Like a slug, like a snake on the road. Mashed him. Then brought the tar sprayer down the hill. Covered what was left. Now he is the road."

"Good god! How can you be certain of this?"

But he knew that she *was* certain. And this was what the group had wanted of her: this vision, this insight. And this was the means they had taken to enforce their demand.

"I suppose you could instruct the road authorities to take up the surface again," she said scornfully. "Then what?"

"But it is atrocious!"

"Oh—" She shrugged. "In the old days, when there were gods, somebody was always sacrificed for a new road or building. Was it not so?"

"But you, mademoiselle? Are you safe with what you know and what they want?"

Again she shrugged. "Who is safe, ever? But they know I can strike back. That is what keeps them in check. Now, here our ways part, Inspector. Good day to you. The police office is there, straight ahead."

She walked away with her basket to a row of market stalls.

In the small police office the local agent, Monsieur Thénard, welcomed the inspector politely.

"Tell me about that group of young men, the Herons," suggested Vidame.

"Oh, they are a kind of brotherhood. I believe the group has existed in this town for many, many years. I am a Rennes man myself," explained Thénard. "At first I believed them to be harmless enough, but now I am inclined to suspect they have had a hand in various robberies that have taken place in the province during the last few years, crimes with a certain stamp of audacity and wildness. But there is no proving anything, and they confine their activities to places a long way from home. They travel great distances on their motorbikes."

"Would you have anything to connect them with the disappearance of Jacques Dodman?"

"Ah, I see you have heard the local talk. But no, I have nothing concrete to go on, nothing."

Vidame thought of the scene that Daniella had enabled him to witness. But he could not mention something so fantastic to this colleague.

"Tell me about the Dodman family," he said instead.

"They are not popular. People believe there is something unhuman about them. In the old days they would have been burned as witches. 'Their ancestor came up out of the sea,' an old woman said to me. 'Better they should go back and live with him. They are not of our kind.' The mother is not quite—" He tapped his forehead. "You know, of course, about the grandmother—La Daniella?" Vidame nodded. "They say that four out of every five men who watched her performance either died violently or went mad."

"But what did she do?"

"Ah, nobody would ever tell, precisely. That was part of its enticement. The performance was a secret, a kind of initiation ceremony, you might say. I looked her up in reference books relating to Paris theater of the early 1900s. All I learned was, 'Her celebrated act, which took place in the dark, using phosphorescent properties, is now thought to have been semihypnotic; and she was said to have had luminous eyes.' "

"Luminous eyes!" Vidame thought of the present-day Daniella's tinted glasses. He said, "What about the boy, Jacques?"

"Ah, he was just a poor thing, a bit simple, like the mother. He longed to join the Herons—that was his great ambition—but they would never have him."

"No, it is the sister they want, I fancy," remarked Vidame.

Thénard shot him a glance of respect.

"To look through the walls of banks, perhaps?"

"Or merely as a trophy, a mascot?"

Thénard said, "She would never consent."

Since Vidame agreed and since he was quite certain that he would never be able to persuade the town authorities to take up two miles of recently tarred road surface, he returned to Paris a couple of days later. The disappearance of Jacques Dodman was officially filed as an unexplained small-town mystery. Brittany was full of such happenings.

Nevertheless, unsatisfied curiosity kept pricking Vidame to such a degree that he decided to return to Zinzac for the midsummer festivities. It was a pleasant enough place, he told himself. It would be interesting to see it in its high summer season.

In fact, when he arrived, he discovered that both the two small hotels were full to capacity. At last, with no particular enthusiasm, he found himself knocking on the blistered door of Madame Dodman's island guest house.

She had not changed in the least. It might have been the same soiled apron on which she wiped her hands before closing the door. She did not appear to recognize him.

"A room? Monsieur requires a room? But yes, we have just the one left."

The room was meagerly furnished and not overclean, but these defects were in some degree compensated for by the sound of rushing water and the two windows looking out on the divided river.

"Thank you, madame, this will do very well."

"Shall you wish to dine?" she inquired wanly, but he shook his head. He did not trust her cooking.

Venturing into the town later in search of a meal, he found that Zinzac was thoroughly *en fête*. Bunting fluttered around the bandstand; girls were dressed in local costume with large flapping lace bonnets; people danced in the street; and there were stalls selling crêpes, mead, and mysterious local drinks and delicacies. Signs on trees announced the famous Cliff Race at midnight, conducted by the well-known Heron Club on their motorbikes.

Vidame, returning to his room for an evening nap before witnessing this event, again encountered Madame Dodman.

"I—I trust your daughter is well, madame?" he asked with some misgivings.

"Thank you, yes, monsieur," she replied vaguely. "She is out in the town. . . ."

But the inspector had not seen her anywhere.

When he woke, he took a fancy to walk out to the end of the breakwater, which was long and curved to protect the otherwise somewhat inadequate harbor. No one else was there at this hour on a *fête* day. The natives were all celebrating in the town.

But then, at the far, seaward tip, he realized that what he had taken for a post was, in fact, a human figure, kneeling or crouching on the cobbled footway, looking into the water. As he drew near, the figure rose to its feet, and he recognized Daniella. What could she have been doing? Searching for something she had dropped off the breakwater? The sea had darkened to the deep slate-blue that comes with twilight; oily calm, it stirred in smooth shellback curves, except for an idle swirl at the end of the breakwater, which might be from the suck of the water around the angle of the stonework. Or it might, thought the inspector fancifully, be an eddy as some huge sea creature sank silently below the surface.

"Good evening, mademoiselle!" he greeted Daniella politely. "I have returned to Zinzac, as you see, for the festivities. And I am still hoping to make some discovery relative to your brother's disappearance."

"It is of no consequence now," she said in a hurried manner. "He is gone. We are reconciled to his loss. Pray do not trouble yourself further in the matter, monsieur."

"But—to bring the perpetrators to justice. . . ."

"Justice is always done in the end. Think of the thrush," she said oddly. A bell began to ring in the town, and she said, "I must leave you now, monsieur. Enjoy your visit."

"Shall I escort you?"

"Oh, no. No, thank you." And she almost ran away from him along the pier.

He followed, curious to know where she was going so fast, but by the time he reached the harborside, she was nowhere to be seen.

Restlessly he walked the narrow, crowded streets, listening to raucous music, jazz, and earlier, more primitive strains, played on accordions, bagpipes, zithers, and uncouth instruments of which he did not know the names. He looked at sideshows, watched the dancers, listened to singers in cafés, but all the time a kind of feverish curiosity drove him on and upward, to where the last and highest houses clung like limpets to the overhanging rock. There the town was darker and quieter. Most of the action was concentrated down by the harbor.

But he did hear the faint sound of bagpipes proceeding from a smallish store—building—some kind of chapel, or legionnaires' hall, he thought it might be—

and he noticed a dim blue light flickering in its windows. He tried the door. It was locked.

Curiosity now completely overwhelmed Inspector Vidame. There must be a way in somehow, or a means of looking in through a window! He strode along beside the building, which stood close to the cliff, with only a narrow alley at the rear separating it from the rock wall. In this alley ten or eleven motorbikes were parked, hidden out of view from the road.

Motorbikes!

Using immense caution, Vidame clambered on to the saddle of one of them and, standing thus, was just able to peer in through the high window.

The interior was almost dark, but after a moment or two he could distinguish a group of figures, perhaps a dozen, squatting on the floor. And then, in the distance, he saw swirls of luminosity, which, as his eyes grew more accustomed, he saw to be a person—a dancer—who seemed to wear nothing but a series of glowing veils. She knelt, rose, twisted, struck slow attitudes, then rapidly twirled and pirouetted. She leaned forward, spun around, balanced, bowed, and swayed. Was it Daniella? It must be!

He could not see her face, though. Only a black oval was visible, framed in the luminous coif.

The audience were motionless, as if hypnotized.

Then the dancer slowly lifted her hands to her head and held them a moment, on either side of her face, before sharply bringing them forward. Suddenly two points of glowing blue could be seen—her *eyes?* But they seemed to be six inches in front of her face. Now they moved to the side, then upward; like butterflies, they hovered near her head.

How the devil does she do it? Vidame asked himself,

and then his precarious perch on the motorbike saddle
was disturbed. The bike fell one way and he another,
bruising himself on the rock face.

By the time he had scrambled up, the dance seemed to
be over. He heard the hall door open and footsteps outside. Had they heard him? No, they appeared to be talking normally enough.

Anxious not to be discovered, Vidame slipped into a
niche of the rock. He saw a dozen dark figures—the
Herons?—flock around to the side of the chapel and
wheel out their motorbikes.

Their voices were awed, subdued.

"Some show, eh?"

"You don't see one like that every day."

"Who is going to *take* her?" somebody called.

"Orthon. He is the leader."

"Yes, Orthon should," they all agreed.

Then he heard Daniella's voice.

"But I do not want to go! That was not part of the
bargain. I have danced for you. That is enough."

"No, no, mademoiselle. You must not leave us yet,"
said a rich, rough voice with a mocking hint of courtesy.

A shorter figure—Daniella, he supposed—was cere-
monially escorted by two of the others, who wore black
hoods.

And then, just for a moment, Vidame had a glimpse of
her eyes, sapphire blue, weaving this way and that, agitat-
edly, before she drew them in.

The warm engines roared into life, and the bikes
blazed off. Vidame ran downhill to the police station, but
he became lost in the narrow mazes of the town. By the
time he had found his way and was urgently talking to
Thénard, the hands of the clock pointed to midnight.

"They go first along the coast road to Pins," Thénard

told him, "then back over the moor so as to begin their first lap at the top of the hill. Ah, there they are now. Look!" He pointed upward. The two men were standing in the street outside the police station. Vidame looked at the cliff face and saw a cascade of lights, two by two, shoot down the first diagonal, turn at the bend like ricocheting tracer bullets, and pour in line down the second lap.

But at the second bend, instead of turning again, they shot outward, still two by two. The sky was suddenly full of descending, twisting sparks.

"Merciful heavens!" Thénard gasped. "They will crash straight down on to the esplanade! Or into the harbor!" He bolted inside to his telephone.

But Vidame waited and watched and thought he saw, among the cloud of falling lights, two tiny blue sparks like twin sapphires.

The next day the local paper reported a terrible fatality. All the Herons had been wiped out by crashing from the cliff clear into the harbor. And the cause, for which the town authorities were at a loss to account, was that the road, though inspected and pronounced in excellent condition at eleven thirty P.M., had somehow, subsequent to that, been smeared for two thirds of its length with a thick coating of slime.

"It was the strangest thing I have ever seen," commented the mayor, called to the scene of the disaster. "It was as if a giant snail had crawled up the Corniche." The newspaper gave no account of a girl being found among the shattered bodies. But Daniella did not return that night; nor was she to be seen the next day.

Inspector Vidame, traveling homeward in the train,

thought, Perhaps she did not want to live. After she had danced for them, she no longer cared what happened.

He began to smile, remembering that dance, and presently his smile changed to a reminiscent laugh, which made the other occupants of the railway carriage eye him rather nervously and wonder if they should move to another compartment.

Old Fillikin

⮜◈◈◈⮞

Miss Evans, the math teacher, had thick white skin, pocked like a nutmeg grater; her lips were pale and thick, often puffed out with annoyance; her thick hair was the drab color of old straw that has gone musty; and her eyes, behind thick glass lenses, stared angrily at Timothy.

"Timothy, how often have I *told* you?" she said. "You have got to show your working. Even if these were the right answers—which they are not—I should give you no marks for them, because no working is shown. How, may I ask, did you arrive at this answer?"

Her felt-tip pen made two angry red circles on the page. All Timothy's neat layout—and the problems were tidily and beautifully set out, at least—all that neat arrangement had been spoiled by a forest of furious red X's, underlinings, and crossings-out that went from top to bottom of the page, with a big *W* for Wrong beside each answer. The page was horrible now—like a scarred face, like a wrecked garden. Timothy could hardly bear to look at it.

"Well? How did you get that answer? Do you *understand* what I'm asking you?"

The trouble was that when she asked him a sharp question like that, in her flat, loud voice, with its aggressive north-country vowels—*an*swer, *ask,* with a short *a* as in grab or bash—he felt as if she were hammering little sharp nails into his brain. At once all his wits completely deserted him, the inside of his head was a blank numbness, empty and echoing like a hollow pot, as if his intelligence had escaped through the holes she had hammered.

"I don't know," he faltered.

"You *don't know?* How can you not *know?* You must have got those answers *some*how! Or do you just put down any figures that come into your head? If you'd got them *right,* I'd assume you'd copied the answers from somebody else's book—but it's quite plain you didn't do that."

She stared at him in frustrated annoyance, her eyes pinpointed like screw-tips behind the thick glass.

Of course he would not be such a fool as to copy someone else's book. He hardly ever got a sum right. If he had a whole series correct, it would be grounds for instant suspicion.

"Well, as you have this whole set wrong—plainly you haven't grasped the principle at all—I'll just have to set you a new lot. Here—you can start at the beginning of Chapter VIII, page 64, and go as far as page 70."

His heart sank horribly. They were all the same kind—the kind he particularly hated—pages and pages of them. It would take him the whole weekend—and now, late on Friday evening—for she had kept him after class—he was already losing precious time.

"Do you understand? Are you following me? I'd better explain the principle again."

And she was off, explaining; her gravelly voice went on and on, about brackets, bases, logarithms, sines, cosines, goodness knows what, but now, thank heaven, his mind was set free, she was not asking questions, and so he could let his thoughts sail off on a string, like a kite flying higher and higher. . . .

"Well?" she snapped. "Have you got it now?"

"Yes—I think so."

"What have I been saying?"

He looked at her dumbly.

But just then a merciful bell began to ring, for the boarders' supper.

"I've got to go," he gasped, "or I'll miss my bus."

Miss Evans unwillingly gave in.

"Oh, very well. Run along. But you'll *have* to learn this, you know—you'll never pass exams, never get *any*where, unless you do. Even farmers need math. Don't think *I* enjoy trying to force it into your thick head—it's no pleasure to *me* to have to spend time going over it all again and again."

He was gathering his books together—the fat, ink-stained gray textbook, the glossy blue new one, the rough notebook, the green exercise book filled with angry red corrections—horrible things, he loathed the very sight and feel of them. If only he could throw them down the well, burn them, never open them again. Some day he would be free of them.

He hurried out, ran down the steps, tore across the school courtyard. The bus was still waiting beyond the gate; with immense relief he bounded into it and flung himself down on the prickly moquette seat.

If only he could blot Miss Evans and the hateful math

out of his mind for two days; if only he could sit out under the big walnut tree in the orchard and just draw and draw and let his mind fly like a kite, and think of nothing at all but what picture was going to take shape under his pencil, and in what colors, later, he would paint it; but now that plan was spoiled, he would have to work at those horrible problems for hours and hours, with his mind jammed among them, like a mouse caught in some diabolical machinery that it didn't invent and doesn't begin to understand.

The bus stopped at a corner by a bridge, and he got out, climbed a fence, and walked across fields to get to the farm where he lived. There was a way around by a cart track, the way the postman came, but it took longer. The fields smelled of warm hay, and the farmyard of dry earth, and cattle cake, and milk, and tractor oil; a rooster crowed in the orchard, and some ducks quacked close at hand; all these were homely, comforting, familiar things, but now they had no power to comfort him; they were like helpless friends holding out their hands to him as he was dragged away to prison.

"These are *rules,* can't you see?" Miss Evans had stormed at him. "You have to learn them."

"Why?" he wanted to ask. "Who made those rules? How can you be certain they were right? Why do you turn upside down and multiply? Why isn't there any square root of minus one?"

But he never had the courage to ask that kind of question.

The next morning he went out and sat with his books in the orchard, under the big walnut, by the old well. It would have been easier to concentrate indoors, to work on the kitchen table, but the weather was so warm and still that he couldn't bear not to be out of doors. Soon the frosts would begin; already the walnut leaves, yellow as butter, were starting to drift down, and the squashy walnut rinds littered the dry grass and stained his bare feet brown. The nights were drawing in.

For some reason he remembered a hymn his granny used to say to him:

> Every morning the red sun
> Rises warm and bright,
> But the evening soon comes on
> And the dark cold night.

The words had frightened him, he could not say why.

He tried to buckle his mind to his work. "If $r \geqq 4$, r weighings can deal with $2r - 1$ loads—" but his thoughts trickled away like a river in sand. He had been dreaming about his grandmother, who had died two years ago. In his dream they had been here, in the orchard, but it was winter, thick gray frost all over the grass, a fur of frost on every branch and twig and grass-blade. Granny had come out of the house with her old zinc pail to get water from the well.

"Tap water's no good to you," she always used to say. "Never drink water that's passed through metal pipes. It'll line your innards with tin, you'll end up clinking like a moneybox. Besides, tap water's full of those floorides and kloorides and wrigglers they put in it—letting on as it's for your good—hah! I'd not pay a penny for a hundred gallons of the stuff. Well water's served me all my life long, and it'll go on doing. Got some taste to it—not like that nasty flat stuff."

"I'll wind up the bucket for you, Granny," he said, and took hold of the heavy well handle.

"That's me boy! One hundred and eight turns."

"A hundred and eight is nine twelves. Nine tens are

ninety, nine elevens are ninety-nine, nine twelves are a hundred and eight."

"Only in your book, lovie. In mine it's different. We have different ones!"

An ironic smile curved her mouth, she stood with arms folded over her clean blue-and-white print apron while he wound and counted. Eighty-nine, ninety, ninety-one, ninety-two . . .

When he had the dripping, double-cone-shaped well bucket at the top and was going to tilt it, so as to fill her small pail, she had exclaimed, "Well, look who's come up with it! Old Fillikin!"

And that, for some reason, had frightened him so much that he had not dared look into the bucket but dropped it, so that it went clattering back into the well and he woke up.

This seemed odd, remembering the dream in daylight, for he had loved his grandmother dearly. His own mother had died when he was two, and Granny had always looked after him. She had been kind, impatient, talkative, always ready with an apple, a hug, a slice of bread-and-dripping if he was hungry or hurt himself. She was full of unexpected ideas and odd information.

"Husterloo's the wood where Reynard the fox keeps his treasure. If we could find that, I could stop knitting, and *you* could stop thinking. You think too much, for a boy your age.

"The letter *N* is a wriggling eel. His name is No one, and his number is Nine.

"Kings always die standing up, and that's the way I mean to die."

She had, too, standing in the doorway, shouting after the postman, "If you don't bring me a letter tomorrow, I'll write your name on a leaf and shut it in a drawer!"

Some people had thought she was a witch because she talked to herself such a lot, but Timothy found nothing strange about her; he had never been in the least frightened of her.

"Who were you talking to, Granny?" he would say, if he came into the kitchen when she was rattling off one of her monologues.

"I was talking to Old Fillikin," she always answered, just as, when he asked, "What's for dinner, Granny?" she invariably said, "Surprise pie with pickled questions."

"Who's Old Fillikin?" he asked once, and she said, "Old Fillikin's my friend. My familiar friend. Every man has a friend in his sleeve."

"Have I got one, Granny?"

"Of course you have, love. Draw his picture, call him by his name, and he'll come out."

Now, sitting by the well, in the warm, hazy sunshine, Timothy began to wonder what Old Fillikin, Granny's familiar friend, would have looked like if he had existed. The idea was, for some reason, not quite comfortable, and he tried to turn his mind back to his math problem.

"R weighings can deal with $2r - 1$ loads . . ." but somehow the image of Old Fillikin would keep sneaking back among his thoughts, and, almost without noticing that he did so, he began to doodle in his rough notebook.

Old Fillikin fairly leaped out of the page: every stroke, every touch of the point filled him in more swiftly and definitely. Old Fillikin was a kind of hairy frog; he looked soft and squashy to the touch—like a rotten pear, or a damp eiderdown—but he had claws too, and a mouthful of needle-sharp teeth. His eyes were very shrewd—they were a bit like Granny's eyes—but there was a sad, lost look about them too, as there had been about Granny's, as if she were used to being misunderstood. Old Fillikin was not a creature that you would want to meet in a narrow high-banked lane with dusk falling. At first Timothy was not certain of his size. Was he as big as an apple, so that he could float, bobbing, in a bucket drawn up from a well, or was he, perhaps, about the size of Bella the Tamworth sow? The pencil answered that question, sketching in a gate behind Old Fillikin, which showed that he was at least two feet high.

"Ugh!" said Timothy, quite upset at his own creation, and he tore out the page from his notebook, crumpled it up, and dropped it down the well.

$$\frac{dy}{dx} = \lim_{dx \to 0} \frac{f(x + dx) - f(x)}{x}$$

"Numbers!" he remembered Granny scoffing, years ago, when he was hopelessly bogged down in his seven-times table. "Some people think they can manage everything by numbers. As if they were set in the ground like bricks!"

"How do you mean, Granny?"

"As if you daren't slip through between!"

"But how *can* you slip between them, Granny? There's nothing between one and two—except one and a half."

"You think there's only one lot of numbers?"

"Of course! One, two, three, four, five, six, seven, eight, nine, ten. Or in French," he said grandly, "it's *un, deux, trois—*"

"Hah!" she said. "Numbers are just a set of rules that some bonehead made up. They're just the fence he built to keep fools from falling over the edge."

"What edge?"

"Oh, go and fetch me a bunch of parsley from the garden!"

That was her way of shutting him up when she'd had enough. She liked long spells by herself, did Granny, though she was always pleased to see him again when he came back.

"*The arrow* → tends to a given value as a limit . . ."

"Timothy!" called his father. "Aunt Di says it's lunchtime."

"Okay! Coming!"

"Did I see you drop a bit of paper down the well just now?"

"Yes, I did," he admitted, rather ashamed.

"Well, don't! Just because we don't drink the water doesn't mean that well can be used as a rubbish dump. After dinner you go and fish it out."

"Sorry, Dad."

During the meal his father and Aunt Di were talking about a local court case: a man who had encouraged, indeed trained, his dog to go next door and harass the neighbors, bite their children, and dig holes in their flowerbeds. The court had ordered the dog to be destroyed. Aunt Di, a dog lover, was indignant about this.

"It wasn't the dog's fault! It was the owner. They should have had *him* destroyed—or sent him to prison!"

If I had a dog, thought Timothy, I could train it to go and wake Miss Evans every night by barking under her window, so that she'd fall asleep in class. Or it could get in through her cat door and pull her out of bed . . .

"Wake up, boy, you're half asleep," said his father. "It's all that mooning over schoolbooks, if you ask me. You'd better come and help me cart feed this afternoon."

"I've got to finish my math first. There's still loads to do."

"They give them too much homework, if you ask *me*," said Aunt Di. "Addles their minds."

"Well, you get that bit of paper out of the well, anyway," said his father.

He could see it, glimmering white down below; it had caught on top of the bucket, which still hung there, though nobody used it. He had quite a struggle to wind it up—the handle badly needed oiling and shrieked at every turn. At last, leaning down, he was able to grab the crumpled sheet; then he let go of the handle, which whirled around crazily as the bucket rattled down again.

But, strangely enough, the crumpled sheet was blank. Timothy felt half relieved, half disappointed; he had been curious to see if his drawing of Old Fillikin was as nasty as he had remembered. Could he have crumpled up the wrong sheet? But no other had a picture on it. At last he decided that the damp atmosphere in the well must have faded the pencil marks. The paper felt cold, soft, and pulpy—rather unpleasant. He carried it indoors and poked it into the kitchen coal stove.

Then he did another hour's work indoors, scrambling through the problems somehow, anyhow. Miss Evans would be angry again, they were certain to be wrong— but, for heaven's sake, he couldn't spend the whole of Saturday at the horrible task. He checked the results, where it was possible to do so, on his little pocket calculator; blessed, useful little thing, it came up with the results so humbly and willingly, flashing out solutions far faster than his mind could. Farmers need math too, he remembered Miss Evans saying; but when I'm a farmer, he resolved, I shall have a computer to do all those jobs, and I'll just keep to the practical work.

Then he was free, and his father let him drive the tractor, which of course was illegal, but he had been doing it since he was ten and drove better than Kenny the cowman. "You can't keep all the laws," his father said. "Some just have to be broken. All farmers' sons drive tractors. Law's simply a system invented to protect fools," as Granny had said about the numbers.

That night Timothy dreamed that Old Fillikin came up out of the well and went hopping and flopping away across the fields in the direction of Markhurst Green, where Miss Evans lived. Timothy followed in his dream and saw the ungainly yet agile creature clamber in through the cat door. *"Don't!* Oh, please, *don't!"* he tried to call. "I didn't mean—I never meant *that*—"

He could hear the flip-flop as it went up the stairs, and he woke himself, screaming, in a tangle of sheet and blanket.

On Sunday night the dream was even worse. That night he took his little calculator to bed with him and made it work out the nine-times table until there were no more places on the screen.

Then he recited Granny's hymn: "Every morning the red sun/Rises warm and bright,/But the evening soon comes on/And the dark cold night."

If only I could stop my mind working, he thought. He remembered Granny saying, "If we could find Reynard's treasure in Husterloo wood, *I* could stop knitting, and *you* could stop thinking." He remembered her saying, "Kings die standing, that's the way I mean to die."

At last he fell into a light, troubled sleep.

On Mondays, math was the first period, an hour and a half. He had been dreading it, but in another way he was desperately anxious to see Miss Evans, to make sure that she was all right. In his second dream, Old Fillikin had pushed through her bedroom door, which stood ajar, and hopped across the floor. Then there had been a kind of silence filled with little fumbling sounds; then a most blood-curdling scream—like the well handle, as the bucket rattled down.

It was only a dream, Timothy kept telling himself as he rode to school on the bus; nothing but a dream.

But the math class was taken by Mr. Gillespie. Miss Evans, they heard, had not come in. And, later, the school grapevine passed along the news. Miss Evans had suffered a heart attack last night; died before she could be taken to the hospital.

When he got off the bus that evening and began to cross the dusk-filled fields toward home, Timothy walked faster than usual and looked warily about him.

Where—he could not help wondering—was Old Fillikin now?

Snow Horse

❧❧❧

A pleasant place, the Forest Lodge Inn seemed as you rode up the mountain track, with its big thatched barns and stables all around, the slate-paved courtyard in front, and the solidity of the stone house itself, promising comfort and good cheer. But inside, there was a queer chill; guests could never get warm enough in bed, pile on however so many blankets they might; the wind whispered uneasily around the corners of the building, birds never nested in its eaves, and travelers who spent a night there somehow never cared to come back for another.

Summertime was different. People would come for the day, then, for the pony-trekking; McGall, the innkeeper, kept thirty ponies, sturdy little mountain beasts, and parties would be going out every morning, all summer long, over the mountains, taking their lunch with them in knapsacks and returning at night tired and cheerful; then the Forest Lodge was lively enough. But in winter, after the first snow fell, scanty at first, barely covering the grass, then thicker and thicker till Glenmarrich Pass was blocked and for months no one could come up from the town below—ah, in winter the inn was cold, grim, and silent indeed. McGall tried many times to persuade the Tourist Board to install a ski lift on Ben Marrich, but the board members were not interested in McGall's profits, they wanted to keep their tourists alive; they said there were too many cliffs and gullies on the mountain for safe skiing. So between November and March most of the ponies would go down to Loch Dune to graze in its watermeadows, where the sea winds kept the snow away; others drowsed and grew fat in the big thatched stables.

Who looked after them? Cal did, the boy who had been fished out of a snowdrift thirteen years before, a hungrily crying baby wrapped in a sheepskin jacket. Both his parents, poor young things, lay stiff and dead by him, and not a scrap of paper on them to show who they were. Nobody came forward to claim the baby, who, it turned out, was lame from frostbite; McGall's wife, a good-natured woman, said she'd keep the child. But her own boy, Dirk, never took to the foundling, nor did his father. After Mrs. McGall died of lung trouble, young Cal had a hard time of it. Still, by then he had proved his usefulness, did more than half the work in stable and yard, and as he was never paid a penny, McGall found it handy to keep him on. He ate scraps, got bawled at, was cuffed about the head a dozen times a day, and took his comfort in loving the ponies, which, under his care, shone and throve like Derby winners.

Ride them? No, he was never allowed to do that.

"With your lame leg? Forget it," said McGall. "I'll not have my stock ruined by you fooling around on them. If I see you on the back of any of my string, I'll give you such a leathering that you won't be sitting down for a month."

Cal had a humble nature. He accepted that he was not good enough to ride the ponies. Never mind! They all loved the boy who tended them. Each would turn to nuzzle him, blowing sweet warm air through his thatch of straw-yellow hair, as he limped down the stable lines.

On a gusty day in November a one-eyed traveler came riding a gray horse up Glenmarrich Pass.

McGall and Dirk had gone down with the Land-Rover to Glen Dune to buy winter supplies, for the first snows were close ahead; by now the inn was shut up for the season, and Cal was the only soul there, apart from the beasts.

The traveler dismounted halfway up the track and led his plodding gray the rest of the way; poor thing, you could see why, for it was dead lame and hobbled painfully, hanging its head as if in shame. A beautiful dark dapple-gray, it must have been a fine horse once but was now old, thin, sick, and tired; looked as if it had been ridden a long, long way, maybe from the other side of the world. And the rider, leading it gently up the rocky path, eyed it with sorrow and regret, as if he knew, only too well, what its fate would soon be and what had brought that fate about.

Reaching the inn door, the traveler knocked hard on the thick oak with the staff he carried: *rap, rap!* still holding his nag's reins looped over his elbow.

Cal opened the door: a small, thin, frightened boy.

"Mr. McGall's not here, sir! He went down the mountain to buy winter stores. And he told me to let nobody in. The fires are all out. And there's no food cooked."

"It's not food I need," said the traveler. "All I want is a drink. But my horse is lame and sick; he needs rest and care. And I must buy another, or hire one, for I am riding on an urgent errand to a distant place, a long way off on the other side of the mountain."

Cal gazed at the man in doubt and fright. The stranger

was tall, with a gray beard; he wore a blue riding cape and a broad-brimmed hat that was pulled down to conceal the missing eye with its shrunken eyelid; his face was rather stern.

"Sir," Cal said, "I would like to help you but my master will beat me if I let anyone take a horse when he is not here."

"I can pay well," said the one-eyed man. "Just lead me to the stables."

Somehow, without at all meaning to, Cal found that he was leading the traveler around the corner to the stable yard and the long, thick-roofed building where the ponies rested in warmth and comfort. The one-eyed man glanced swiftly along the row and picked out a gray mountain pony that was sturdy and trim, though nothing like so handsome as his own must once have been.

"This one will serve me," said he. "I will pay your master ten gold pieces for it"—which he counted out, from a goatskin pouch. Cal's eyes nearly started from his head; he had never seen gold money before. Each coin must be worth hundreds of pounds.

"Now fetch a bucket of warm mash for my poor beast," said the traveler.

Eagerly Cal lit a brazier, heated water, put bran into the mash, and some wine too, certain that his master would not grudge it to a customer who paid so well. The sick horse was too tired to take more than a few mouthfuls, though its master fed it and gentled it himself. Then Cal rubbed it down and buckled a warm blanket around its belly.

Watching with approval, the stranger said, "I can see that you will take good care of my gray. And I am glad of that, for he has been my faithful friend for more years than you have hairs on your head. Look after him well!

And if, by sad fortune, he should die, I wish you to bury him out on the mountain under a rowan tree. But first take three hairs from his mane. Two of them you will give to me, when we meet again; tie the third around your wrist for luck. If Gray does not die, I will come back for him."

"How will you know that he is alive, sir?"

The one-eyed man did not answer that question but said, "Here is another gold piece to pay for his board."

"It is too much, sir," objected Cal, trembling, for there was something about the stranger's voice that echoed through and through his head, like the boom of a waterfall.

"Too much? For my faithful companion?"

Cal flinched at his tone; but the man smiled.

"I can see that you are an honest boy. What is your name?"

"Cal, sir."

"Look after my horse kindly, Cal. Now I must be on my way, for time presses. But first bring me a drink of mead."

Cal ran into the house and came back with the inn's largest beaker brimful of homemade mead, which was powerful as the midsummer sun. The traveler, who had been murmuring words of parting to his horse, drank off the mead in one gulp, then kissed his steed on its soft gray nose.

"Farewell, old friend. We shall meet in another world, if not in this."

He flung a leg over the fresh pony, shook up the reins, and galloped swiftly away into the thick of a dark cloud that hung in the head of the pass.

His own horse lifted up its drooping head and let out

one piercing cry of sorrow that echoed far beyond the inn buildings.

McGall, driving back up the valley with a load of stores, heard the cry. "What the deuce was that?" he said. "I hope that lame layabout has not been up to mischief."

"Stealing a ride when he shouldn't?" suggested Dirk as the Land-Rover bounced into the stable yard.

Of course McGall was angry, very angry indeed, when he found that a useful weight-carrying gray pony was gone from his stable, in exchange for a sad, sick beast with hardly more flesh on its bones than a skeleton.

Cal made haste to give him the eleven gold coins, and he stared at them hard, bit them, tested them over a candle, and demanded a description of the stranger.

"A one-eyed fellow with a broad-brimmed hat and blue cape? Nobody from these parts. Didn't give his name? Probably an escaped convict. What sort of payment is *that?* I've never seen such coins. How dare you let that thief make off with one of my best hacks?"

Cal was rewarded by a stunning blow on each side of the head and a shower of kicks.

"Now I have to go down into town again to show these coins to the bank, and it's all your fault, you little no-good. And I'm not giving stable room and good fodder to that spavined cripple. It can go out in the bothy. And strip that blanket off it!"

The bothy was a miserable tumbledown shed, open on two sides to the weather. Cal dared not argue with his master—that would only have earned him another beating or a tooth knocked out—but he did his best to shelter the sick horse with bales of straw, and he strapped on it the tattered moth-eaten cover from his own bed. Forbidden to feed the beast, he took it his own meals, and he huddled beside it at night, to give it the warmth of his own body. But the gray would eat little and drink only a few mouthfuls of water. And after three days it died, from grieving for its master, Cal thought, rather than sickness.

"Good riddance," said the innkeeper, who by that time had taken the gold pieces to the bank and been told that they were worth an amazing amount of money. He kicked the gray horse's carcass. "That's too skinny to use even for dogmeat. Bury it under the stable muck in the corner; it will do to fertilize the crops next summer."

"But," said Cal, "its owner told me, if it died, to bury it under a rowan tree."

"Get out of my sight! Bury it under a rowan—what next? Go and muck out the stables, before I give you a taste of my boot."

So the body of the gray horse was laid under a great pile of straw and stable sweepings. But before this, Cal took three hairs from its mane. One he tied around his wrist, the other two he folded in a paper and kept always in his pocket.

A year went by, and the one-eyed traveler never returned to inquire after his horse.

He must have known that it died, thought Cal.

"I knew he'd never come back," said McGall. "Ten to one those coins were stolen. It's lucky I changed them right away."

When spring came, the heap of stable sweepings was carted out and spread over the steep mountain pastures. There, at the bottom of the pile, lay the bones of the dead horse, and they had turned black and glistening as coal. Cal managed to smuggle them away, and he buried them, at night, under a rowan tree.

That autumn, snow fell early, with bitter, scouring

winds, so that from September onward no more travelers took the steep track up to the Forest Lodge. McGall grew surlier than ever, thinking of the beasts to feed and no money coming in; he cursed Cal for the slightest fault and kept him hard at work leading the ponies around the yard to exercise them.

"Lead them, don't ride them!" shouted McGall. "Don't let me see you on the backs of any of those ponies, cripple! Why the deuce didn't you die in the blizzard with your wretched parents?"

Secretly Cal did not see why his lame leg should prevent his being able to sit on a horse. Night after night he dreamed of riding the mounts that he tended with such care: the black, piebald, roan, bay, gray, chestnut; when they turned to greet him as he brought their feed he would hug them and murmur, "Ah, you'd carry me, wouldn't you, if I was allowed?" In his dreams he was not lame. In his dreams a splendid horse, fiery, swift, obedient to his lightest touch, would carry him over the mountain wherever he wanted to go.

When winter set in, only six ponies were left in the stable; the rest had been taken down to the lowland pasture. But now a series of accidents reduced these remaining: the black threw McGall when he was out searching for a lost sheep and galloped into a gully and broke its neck; the chestnut escaped from Dirk as he was tightening its shoe in the smithy and ran out onto the mountain and was seen no more; the roan and gray fell sick and lay with heaving sides and closed eyes, refusing to eat, until they died. Cal grieved for them sadly.

And, day after day, snow fell, until a ten-foot drift lay piled against the yard gate. The inmates of Forest Lodge had little to do; Cal's care of the two remaining ponies took only an hour or two each day. Dirk sulked indoors by the fire; McGall, angry and silent, drank more and more mead. Quarrelsome with drink, he continually abused Cal.

"Find something useful to do! Shovel the snow out of the front yard; suppose a traveler came by; how could he find the door? Get outside, and don't let me see your face till suppertime."

Cal knew that no traveler would come, but he was glad to get outside, and took broom and shovel to the front yard. Here the wind, raking over the mountain, had turned the snow hard as marble. It was too hard to shift with a broom; Cal had to dig it away in blocks. These he piled up on the slope outside the yard, until he had an enormous rugged mound. At last a way was cut to the front door—supposing that any foolhardy wayfarer should brave the hills in such weather.

Knowing that if he went back indoors McGall would only find some other pointless task, Cal used the blade of his shovel to carve the pile of frozen snow into the rough shape of a horse. Who should know better than he how a horse was shaped? He gave it a broad chest, a small proud head pulled back alertly on the strong neck, and a well-muscled rump. The legs were a problem, for snow legs might not be strong enough to support the massive body he had made, so he left the horse rising out of a block of snow and carved the suggestion of four legs on each side of the block. And he made a snow saddle, but no bridle or stirrups.

"There now!" He patted his creation affectionately. "When we are all asleep, you can gallop off into the dark and find that one-eyed traveler, and tell him that I cared for his gray as well as I could, but I think its heart broke when his master left it."

The front door opened and Dirk put his head out.

"Come in, no-good," he yelled, "and peel the spuds for supper!"

Then he saw the snow horse and burst into a rude laugh.

"Mustn't ride the stock, so he makes himself a snow horsie. Bye, bye, baby boy, ride nice snow horsie, then!" He walked round the statue and laughed even louder. "Why, it has *eight legs!* Who in the world ever heard of a horse with eight legs? Dad! Dad, come out here and see what Useless has been doing!"

McGall, half tipsy, had roamed into the stables and was looking over the tack to see what needed mending. At Dirk's shout he blundered hastily out into the yard, knocking over in his heedless hurry the lighted lantern he had set on a shelf.

He stared angrily at Cal's carved horse.

"Is that how you've been wasting your time? Get inside, fool, and make the meal!"

Then smoke began to drift around the corner, and a loud sound of crackling.

"Lord above, Dad, you've gone and set fire to the stable!" cried Dirk.

Aghast, they all raced round to the stable block, which was burning fiercely.

What water they had, in tubs or barrels, was frozen hard; there was no possible way to put out the blaze. Cal did manage to rescue the bay horse, but the piebald, which was old, had breathed too much smoke, and staggered and fell back into the fire; and the bay, terrified of the flames, snapped the halter with which it had been tethered in the cowshed and ran away over the mountain and was lost.

The whole stable block was soon reduced to a black

shell; if the wind had not blown the flames in the other direction, the inn would have burned too.

McGall, in rage and despair, turned on Cal.

"This is your fault, you little rat!"

"Why, master," said Cal, dumbfounded, "I wasn't even there!"

"You bring nothing but bad luck! First my wife died, now I haven't a horse left, and my stable's ashes. Get out! I never want to see your face again!"

"But—master—how *can* I go? It's nearly dark—it's starting to snow again. . . ."

"Why should I care? You can't stay here. You made yourself a snow horse," said McGall, "you can ride away on that—ride it over a cliff, and that'll be good riddance."

He stamped off indoors. Dirk, pausing only to shout mockingly, "Ride the snow horsie, baby boy!" followed him, slamming and bolting the door behind him.

Cal turned away. What could he do? The wind was rising; long ribbons of snow came flying on its wings. The stable was burned; he could not shelter there. His heart was heavy at the thought of all the horses he had cared for, gone now. With slow steps he moved across the yard to the massive snow horse and laid an arm over its freezing shoulder.

"You are the only one I have left now," he told it. And he took off his wrist the long hair from the mane of the traveler's gray and tied the hair around the snow horse's neck. Then, piling himself blocks of snow for a mounting block, since this was no pony but a full-sized horse, he clambered up on to its back.

Dusk had fallen; the inn could no longer be seen. Indeed, he could hardly make out the white form under him. He could feel its utter cold, though, striking up all through his own body—and, with the cold, a feeling of tremendous power, like that of the wind itself. Then—after a moment—he could feel the snow horse begin to move and tingle with aliveness, with a cold wild thrilling life of its own. He could feel its eight legs begin to stamp and stretch and strike the ground.

Then they began to gallop.

When McGall rose next morning, sober and bloodshot-eyed and rather ashamed of himself, the very first thing he did was to open the front door.

More snow had fallen during the night; the path Cal had dug to the gate yesterday was filled in again, nine inches deep.

A line of footprints led through this new snow to the inn door—led right up to the door, as if somebody had walked to the doorstep and stood there without moving for a long time, thinking or listening.

"That's mighty queer," said McGall, scratching his head. "Someone must have come to the door—but he never knocked, or we'd have heard him. He never came in. Where the devil did he go?"

For there was only *one* line of footprints. None led off again.

"He was a big fellow too," said McGall. "That print is half as long again as my foot. Where did the fellow go? Where did he come from? I don't like it."

But how the visitor had come, how he had gone, remained a mystery. As for Cal, he was gone too, and the snow horse with him. Where it had stood there was only a rough bare patch, already covered by new snow.

The Hunchback
of Brook Green

≈≈≈

I can still remember my Uncle Emile's house in London.
He was not really my uncle, but my father's second
cousin; they were partners in our family firm of Bouvard
Frères, wine shippers. Uncle Emile took care of the London end of the firm, and every two years of my childhood, from four on, I was sent from Provence to spend
three months with him (my mother had died at my birth,
so the arrangement may have been convenient for my
father) in order to acquire fluent English and learn the
overseas side of the business. For the first few visits I
learned more about Uncle Emile than about the firm. He
was a thin, lively, elegant man, very fastidious, with a
wide range of knowledge and a fondness for jokes; I
loved him dearly.

On those early visits I was looked after by my uncle's
housekeeper, Mrs. Emerald—a kind, silent, melancholy
woman. I think she mutely loved Emile; she would have
done anything for him, and died, for no ascertainable

reason, two months after his death. When I was four she taught me how to make wallets from two pieces of cardboard and three pieces of ribbon—they would open at either side and seemed magical to me. I carried six of them back as presents for my father. In her sunny kitchen I played with the cat, Ejot, and we ate our déjeuner in the little garden with the pear tree; or I walked with her around Brook Green, which, to me, was large as the Camargue, and as mysterious.

Occasionally we would ride on a number-eleven bus all the way across London to Emile's office in Camomile Street, in the heart of the City. The trip seemed to last all day and I thought it wonderful. We always sat upstairs, I beside the window, absorbed, as we surged along, by the sights of London: Chelsea and Pimlico, Victoria Street, embroidered with traffic lights, Westminster Abbey and the Houses of Parliament, Whitehall, where I would see magnificent soldiers in bearskin hats, past Trafalgar Square and Charing Cross, through the narrow Strand and narrower Fleet Street with their ancient buildings and churches, up Ludgate Hill to St. Paul's, and so into the City itself. The number-eleven bus ride has always seemed to me to offer the whole essence of London.

At the office, Uncle Emile, after regaling us with sips of Monbazillac or Framboise, would accompany us back to Brook Green, again on the bus. When we were lucky, the conductress would be our favorite, a laughing blue-eyed girl, with the superb name of Rose Nightingale, who wore her brown hair in a plaited crown on top of her head, darted up and down the bus stairs with the speed of a squirrel, and taught me the game of Lucky Tickets.

In those days the bus tickets were individual oblongs from a charming little rack of them that the conductor carried slung on a strap around the neck. Tickets came in different colors, white for a penny, pink for twopence, and so on, up to the exciting and glamorous higher fares, orange, blue, green, and magenta. Each ticket bore on it two letters and four numbers. In the ticket game, which Rose taught me (and Uncle Emile), you studied the combination of letters and numbers on your ticket, then worked out an omen from them. First you added the numbers together. It was considered lucky if the digits were all the same, or if there were only two different—say, 6333. Having added your numbers, you found the letter of the alphabet that represented the total. Emile taught me a mnemonic, EJOT, for the fifth, tenth, fifteenth, and twentieth letters. (This was why the cat was called Ejot, which Emile pronounced in the French way, Ehjoh.) Then you joined the letter thus achieved to the two already on the ticket and used the result to form a word. For example, with the ticket LT 5454, the product of the numbers would give you *R*, eighteenth in the alphabet, so you had *RLT* or *LTR*. That might be Royalty, or Later, or Letter.

"It's a lucky ticket," Emile would say triumphantly, "for there are only two numbers, so we shall receive a letter with good news!"

Often the omens were proved right; and if they were not, Emile generally took measures to make them so. He was full of jokes and kindness and cheerfulness.

But when I returned at the age of eight, a great change had come over him. He was still kindly and affectionate, but even I, child that I was, could see that something terrible must have happened. He had not lost his handsome looks or his elegance, but was now thin as a rail and pale as death. Stranger yet, he had completely ceased going out by day; all his business at the office was now transacted during the evening hours, between six and midnight. Then, after he had returned to Brook Green on the eleven bus (which ran all night), he did not go to bed. He had lost the ability to sleep. All our family are light sleepers—I myself never require more than four hours a night—but Uncle Emile needed none. All night he would pace about the big first-floor sitting room. He read, he meditated, he worked, wrote, played soft music on his flute, or talked to me.

For when I discovered this habit of his, chains and shackles would not have kept me in bed. Tiptoeing in, so as not to disturb Mrs. Emerald, I would sit on the sofa in the big bay window, hugging the cat and listening to him talk.

I can remember that room as if I were in it now. There was a large faded Persian carpet in colors of black, blue, and rose; the couch and two massive armchairs upholstered in worn, shabby leather, very comfortable to sprawl out on or curl up in; blue curtains and dim lamps, a great globe of the world, and sagging shelves full of books on two walls. Outside was Brook Green, gray, misty, and mysterious under the streetlights; farther away could be heard the muted roar of late traffic in Hammersmith or Shepherds Bush.

What a bizarre picture of the world I received from Uncle Emile! To this day I hardly know, among my memories of that time, which things he told me and which I dreamed. For sometimes I would fall asleep, listening to his voice, and wake to hear him still talking.

Naturally I had asked Mrs. Emerald why he was now so different, so changed.

"Why doesn't he take me to play ball on the green any more? Why don't we ride on the bus to Camomile Street?"

"Hush, child! Never distress the poor master by asking those questions!"

"No, but I am asking you!"

"It is because of poor Rose."

"Rose?"

Then I remembered the laughing leaf-thin girl on the number-eleven bus who had taught me how to recognize a lucky ticket. "What happened to Rose?"

"She died, poor thing. And it was a dreadful, dreadful grief to the poor master." Mrs. Emerald wiped her own eyes. "Now, be a good child and run away and play with Ejot, and, whatever you do, don't ask your uncle about it."

Awed, I crept away to trail a string for the cat, who chased it with a condescending air. But I kept wondering and asking myself what could have happened. Something in Mrs. Emerald's manner told me that Rose must have died in a very tragic and awful way.

Emile never mentioned her.

Many strange things he did tell me, in the course of those wakeful nights: about a tribe of Laotians in the Philippines called the Hmong, whose dreams are so terrible that often a dreamer may die before he wakes; the fatal dream is called the *bangangut,* and the dreamer's family will say, "Oh, the god of the rocks got him in his sleep," or the god of the trees, or the lake. Emile told me of the strange lines across the landscape in the uplands of Peru, which are only visible from miles up in the air—but who is to read them, up there, save God? And who put them there? Emile told me that if you wish to dream about a person, you must put something connected with them under your pillow; he told me how the Roman Britons used to curse their enemies, getting a priest to write the enemy's name and the curse on a lead scroll and leaving it in the temple of Mercury; he told me Spanish peasants believe if a water rat looks at a girl, she will die. He told me about the Jivaros, headhunters who remove the brains from a skull, insert a hot stone, sew up the lips, and hang the head upside down for a year to prevent the ghost from reentering. He told me that if a baby is crying uncontrollably, a stranger should spit in its face; this will calm it. He told me that an Andean llama will not carry a load of more than a hundred pounds. He told me about the snow tigers of the Sikhote Alin mountains, about the Abominable Snowman, and the fifty-foot-high wave of molasses that rolled through the city of Boston in 1919. All these, and many, many other things he told me. But he never spoke of Rose Nightingale.

One night I was kneeling on the big leather sofa and looking out on to the green, as was my habit, hoping to see the big white owl that nested under the eaves of the Queen's Head pub come coasting down on his nightly search for small prey. But suddenly I saw something much more extraordinary.

"Uncle Emile! A man has just come out of that tree! And he is the most singular man I ever saw!"

"Speak English, child!" For I had unconsciously fallen back into my native tongue.

"No, but do come and see him, Uncle. He walks along bent double, with his chin on his knees. And he is wearing a helmet! And I am certain that he came out of that tree. How could a man come out of a tree?"

But my uncle replied, in a voice containing all the misery and despair in the world:

"There is nobody there."

"But I saw him!"

"You saw *nobody*. Go to bed, child, it is time you were asleep and resting."

My uncle seldom ordered me to bed. At the unwonted sternness in his tone I crept away obediently; but it was a long time before I could compose myself to sleep. Who —or what—was that extraordinary bent shadow of a man? Could I really have seen him at all? And why— whether real or no—had he the power to throw my uncle into such wretchedness?

The next day, as I polished the spoons and forks for her, I told Mrs. Emerald what I had seen. All the blood drained from her face as I described the stooped, grop- ing, helmeted figure that seemed to have emerged from the tree.

"Oh, no! Oh, no!" she panted, aghast and breathless. "He's walking! He's walking! Oh, poor Tom! Oh, the poor master!"

And she threw her apron over her face, while an- guished sobs racked her thin body.

I, of course, heedless child that I was, though I felt pity for this inexplicable grief and trouble, longed, above all else, for some explanation.

"What *is* that creature, Mrs. Emerald? Who is he?"

"He is no one, child," she answered, just as my uncle had done. "There was nobody on the green."

"But he was there! I saw him. I could not have in- vented him!"

"Then you saw a ghost," said Mrs. Emerald, wiping her eyes on her apron. "For the flesh-and-blood part of him, poor marred being that he was, perished long ago. But it's likely enough he'd walk again. Last night, No- vember the fourth, was the anniversary of when it hap- pened."

"What happened? Who was he?"

Realizing, I suppose, that I might go and pester my uncle if she did not allay some part of my ravenous curiosity, Mrs. Emerald at last told me a few details about the hunchback of Brook Green. His name, she said, was Tom Virgoe. She sighed at the name, as if the very essence of her spirit were sucked from her at the mere mention of it.

"He was my nephew," she said. "My poor sister's son."

"But why was he—like that?"

"You know," she said, "that in World War II the Germans had secret weapons. There were two kinds of V-bombs: flying bombs and long-range rockets, both of them fired from bases on the Continent; they fell on London and the country round about."

"Yes," I said, "I knew that."

"As well as those, there was a third weapon, the V-III. Only one was fired off before the Allied armies found the base from which it was launched and destroyed it."

"What was it? What did it do?"

"Only one was fired. That one killed five hundred people and turned twenty streets to a sea of mud—oh, the wicked things that men do to each other!" Mrs. Emerald wiped her eyes again. "But it wasn't ordinary explosive. They never discovered what it was. My poor sister lived in Hemp Street, just outside the bombed area. She wasn't killed at the time, but she died two days later, of shock. That was when Tom was born."

There was something frighteningly grim and sad about her voice. I knew I ought not to ask more questions. But how could I help it? I said, trembling, "What happened to him, Mrs. Emerald?"

"Oh, he grew up," she said. "In his way. He had to have special care. And so did those that looked after him; before they realized that, two or three doctors had died. He had to wear a lead helmet, always, and protective clothing. And live underground."

"*Underground?* Where?"

"Why, here," she said. "Under Brook Green. In the caves."

I had not known there were caves under Brook Green.

"But he's not still there?"

"No. I told you," she said wearily. "He died. If you saw anything, it was his ghost you saw. And who would wonder at it? Poor Tom—poor Tom. He had feelings, the same as anybody else. He wasn't a robot. He made up beautiful songs too. Sometimes I thought he suffered *more* than ordinary folk. Run along, child; go outside and play with your ball. I've told you all you need to know. They're dead, Tom and Rose. It's all over."

So I went out to play ball in Brook Green. Half terrified, half spellbound, I tiptoed around over the area where, last night, that grotesquely bent figure had moved with equal uncertainty over the grass.

Today had the bite of winter. The sun, red as a Bordeaux plum, was just inching its way out of the mists over Ravensbrook Park, and a heavy hoar frost lay silver-gray over the thin winter grass. I began to search for the tree from behind which I had seen the specter of Tom Virgoe emerge. And I found it: a great witch elm, five trees joined into one. It grew on the south side of the green, not far from the Queen's Head pub. Studying it nervously I perceived a small grating beside it in the ground; a grating padlocked into a manhole, with steps under it leading down, apparently under the roots of the tree.

I was peering down through this grating when a policeman strolled up to me.

"Lost your ball?" he inquired.

"No. I just wondered what's under there."

"Goes down to the sewers," he said without hesitation. "And you'd best not hang over it, or bad poisons might

come up and make you sick. Go on—hop it, before I call
your ma. And don't let me see you poking around there
again."

"I haven't got a ma," I said, but just the same I hopped
it. There was something impressively firm about his manner.

Neither at that time nor on subsequent visits did I dare
question Uncle Emile directly about Tom Virgoe, though
I felt certain there must be some connection between
him and the death of poor Rose Nightingale.

Of course at first I spent a good many hours at night,
fascinated, terrified, looking from the front window,
hoping for another glimpse of that doubled-up figure.
Ever since the initial sight, my imagination had been
feverishly occupied with him. *Why* had he been obliged
to live in the caves? What kind of caves were they? A
wine-shipping colleague of Emile's had once taken me to
Chislehurst, and I had visited cellars in the Champagne
region of France. Were the Brook Green caves like that—
a maze of high, gleaming white passages, some burrowed
out by prehistoric man, scraped by flint knives out of the
chalk and filled with furry darkness? How had the hunchback spent his days? Were there animals painted on the
walls, such as I had seen on trips with my father to Mous-
tier and the Lot valley caves?

Sometimes, when I saw the wind blow sycamore leaves
across Brook Green, or the scarlet buses bowling down
Shepherds Bush Road, or white gulls whirling up against
a stormy December sky, I would think of hapless Tom
Virgoe, destined to spend his life in darkness like a mole.

Darkness came early to London these foggy winter
days. By three or four the streetlamps would begin to
glow pink and orange. Now my uncle Emile developed a

new habit, a new eccentricity. As soon as dark fell, out he
would go, not to his office, but to ride back and forth to
the City on a bus. Back and forth, back and forth, as many
as five or six times during one evening.

"Oh, sir! You'll wear yourself to a thread!" I heard
Mrs. Emerald say to him distressfully. "Indeed, indeed
you should not do it."

"I can think best about her on a bus," he answered.
"Remember. Think about her."

Sometimes I rode with him; and I noticed how restlessly, anxiously, ceaselessly, thirstily, he would watch
the buses as we met them coming in the other direction,
peering through the windows. Once he said to me absently, "When two vehicles are traveling in opposite di-
rections, they are bound to meet. Thank God! For if
mine happened to be traveling behind hers—I should
never catch up."

From which I guessed that, as the ghost of Tom
haunted Brook Green, he hoped to find the ghost of
Rose, somewhere between Hammersmith and Liverpool
Street.

On the following visit, when I was ten, one snowy night,
running across the green among spiraling milky flakes,
to post a letter, I heard a voice—an eerily bewitching
high, cold voice that sang, with piercing sweetness, a
song that I vaguely remembered from an earlier period
of my childhood. It had once been popular in France and
Italy; translated into several European languages, like
"Jennifer," heard and sung everywhere:

"Drinking Tio Pepe, thinking about Rose,
That's the way the evening generally goes

Nine, ticks the hour-hand, ten, call the bells;
From eleven through to midnight, I think of
nothing else. . . ."

Had I really heard the voice, or had I imagined it?

I posted my letter—which told my father the date of
my return to France—and fled back to the house in a
sudden frenzy of nervousness. Mrs. Emerald came from
the kitchen, startled at the violence with which I slammed
the front door.

"What's the matter, child?"

"Nothing," I lied.

But the plaintive tune lodged in my head, and a few
days later, thoughtlessly, I began to hum it and then to
sing the words. Uncle Emile abruptly got up (we were at
breakfast) and left the room. And, to my utter astonish-
ment, Mrs. Emerald, the slow-moving, gentle Mrs. Emerald, gave my face a stinging slap.

"Don't ever let me hear you sing that again!" she said.

"Why not?" I gasped, rubbing my burning cheek.

"Tom Virgoe wrote that song!"

"He *wrote* it?"

"I told you. That was how he made a living—poor
creature."

The subject was not mentioned again. The rest of the
visit passed without event, and I was quite sorry to return
to the warmth and placidity of the southern French landscape.

On my next visit, at age twelve, I was half inclined to
believe that I must have imagined the whole story of the
hunchback. Most likely it had been a dream, or several
dreams. The gentle, placid Mrs. Emerald could not have
told me such wild stuff! It had been a product of those

nightly colloquies in the front room with my Uncle Emile, when the bizarre tales he told me began to whirl and whip together in my mind, then brewed and fermented into a heady potion, changing, as in wine production, into something wholly different from the original ingredients. That must be it. I always did have amazing dreams when staying at Brook Green. During those condensed hours of sleep the sounds of London wove through my brain, creating eerie patterns and grotesque tales of which I was the observer more often than the protagonist. And I was glad of this, for the dreams were often so alarming that if I had been personally involved, I would have died of terror, like the Laotians in their *bangangut.*

This visit fell in a summer season, and a hot one, a dreamy, indolent holiday from time; customers sat on metal chairs outside the Queen's Head pub with their beer, dogs flopped panting in the dust; the grass of Brook Green wore a limp, threadbare look, and the whole feeling and tone of the neighborhood had an easy, carefree languor, like that of my native Provence.

Mrs. Emerald and my uncle seemed exactly the same, set in the mold of middle age, like two characters in a familiar tale that one picks up idly in order to reread one's favorite episodes.

One of my amusements, that hot, breezy summer, was drawing pictures of horses, cutting them out of paper, and letting them blow out of the window. I liked to imagine them racing over the green, fluttering like birds through the boughs of trees. I gave them names and invented adventures for them.

This game annoyed my uncle for various reasons. First, he pointed out that it was childish, which it undoubtedly was.

"Have you no better way of occupying your time?"

Second, he said, with justice, that it was untidy and antisocial; my paper horses added to the general mess and litter on the green, where schoolchildren dropped ice-pop papers and their elders left beer cans. Third, it was evidence of stupidity. Had I nothing more interesting in my mind than horses?

"I intend to be a jockey!" I asserted.

This put my uncle in a passion. He favored me with a ten-minute lecture on the folly and vulgarity of harboring such a mindless ambition when there was a family business of impressive tradition and repute awaiting me.

I said, "I shall hire a manager to take care of it!"

Emile never resorted to violence or bad language when he was angry—which was extremely rare. Now he became very much paler than usual, eyed me with compressed lips and nostrils indrawn, then took up his briefcase and left the house. It was eight o'clock in the evening. I saw him cross the green to where the fleet of number-eleven buses waited, on the far side of Shepherds Bush Road, and I was half inclined to run after him and apologize, tell him that I had only been joking.

But Mrs. Emerald said sharply, "There! Now you've upset your uncle. You should think shame, so good to you as he is! Go and tidy up his bed, and then you had better study at your books for a couple of hours."

Humble and shamed, I crept from the room.

Though Emile never slept, he had a bedroom, a little cell-like apartment with a narrow iron cot and a clothes chest. Here he would rest for an hour or so before going off to the City. On this occasion his bed was hardly disturbed; a faint imprint of his head had been left on the pillow. Plumping it up, I discovered a bus ticket underneath.

RS 0005, it said, and I automatically translated this into RSE.

Rose.

"If you want to dream about a person," Emile had said to me, "put some article connected with them, a letter or a photograph, for instance, under your pillow. An Indian doctor told me that."

Uncle Emile wished to dream about Rose. But how could he dream, since he never slept?

When I had completed my two hours' study, I walked out on to the green. From the pub came the sound of music, and I recognized the tune that had come back into favor this summer: *Drinking Tio Pepe, thinking about Rose . . .*

No wonder my uncle was unusually touchy and easily overset these days; the song was to be heard everywhere.

My relationship with Emile was not as harmonious as it had been formerly; perhaps because I was older, no longer a tractable, lovable small child, but an awkward, obstinate middle-sized one. But still, I was angry with myself for teasing him, and I waited on the green to meet him when he came home later that night.

"I am sorry I distressed you, Uncle Emile. I was only fooling. I do not really wish to become a jockey. And I have picked up all the paper horses."

"Eh bien, it is well. We will forget it," he said wearily. "I daresay you feel constricted here in the city. I do myself." He was aging, I suddenly realized; there were deep lines on his brow, and the wings of hair brushed back from his temples had whitened. "Let us take a turn around the green," he said. "It was hot as Gehenna on that bus."

It was no less hot on Brook Green; the night had grown stiflingly oppressive and humid. A thundery overcast sky seemed to hang so low that the apricot-colored lights on the far side of Shepherds Bush Road were mere pinpoints in the gloom; the trees and houses across the green were veiled in obscurity.

"The air is like Vichyssoise," said my uncle.

Sound carried well through the dense air, and from some lategoer on his homeward way came the mocking light-hearted refrain, "Drinking Tio Pepe, thinking about Rose . . ."

"Oh!" cried Emile, standing still. "I cannot endure this for much longer!" He clenched his fists, raised them, and shook them; his face was ghastly pale, beaded with sweat. "I would give all the years of my life—my life, *hein!* —what use is it? I would give it all—all—all—just for one glimpse of her. Just *one!*" Standing there, in the center of the green, he raised his voice and called, *"Rose! Rose! Rose!"* with such a pleading, yearning break in his utterance that my own heart seemed ready to leave my body in sympathy.

There we stood waiting in the middle of the green.

Nobody else was about—or none that could be seen. For the air was now so black and thick that we might have been wrapped in black kapok, or embedded in black aspic; it was difficult to breathe. I felt much afraid, and groped for my uncle's hand. But his fingers were icy cold and gave me little comfort.

Then in the distance I *saw* something: a dim phosphorescent glow. It began to move slowly in our direction. As it very gradually came closer I recognized the bowed, hunched shape that I had seen once before.

Tom Virgoe!

He plodded toward us at a creeping pace, his hands grasping his ankles, his weirdly helmeted head dangling in front of his shins. No sound came from him at all as he approached us at an infinitesimal speed.

I grew deadly afraid, and clutched at Uncle Emile's hand, whispering, "Uncle, oh, please, let's go home—"

But my uncle, turning away from Tom Virgoe, was staring in the opposite direction, and his grip on my hand had tightened to such a rigidity that even if I had wanted to I could not have pulled myself free.

"Rose!" he breathed. "Ah! It *is* Rose. At last!"

Wraithlike, thin as a candle flame, she floated over the grass, which lay limp and ash-colored in the faint shimmer from the streetlamps. It *was* Rose: I recognized her shining eyes, the proud carriage of her head on its slender neck; above all her movement and bearing, quick and lissome as a willow leaf.

"Rose!" my uncle said again. "At last you came!"

She seemed to look at him with compassion, but also with reproach. And I seemed to hear her voice, the tones of which tingled inside my head, rather than affecting my physical hearing.

"Why, *why* do you keep us here? Why do you continually drag us back? Have you no pity for us? You are like a chain, binding us to our graves. Why can you not let us go?"

He groaned. "But, Rose, how can I help it? You are my only love—the only light of my life."

"But I," she answered in that silvery, unearthly tone, "I don't love *you*. Why should I be kept here by your demands, your importunities? It is Tom that I love."

And floating past us in the unnatural dark, she joined the other apparition.

At that my uncle gave vent to a cry, a moan of such despairing anguish that I felt my own throat contract. He let go my hand in order to stumble after the retreating shape of Rose.

"But you must feel *something* for me—*something?* Tom! I

did my best for you once—I helped you—Don't let her leave me altogether—?"

The two shining figures were now side by side, at some distance away, near the big elm.

To my fascinated terror, that of the hunchback slowly began to straighten. Inch by inch he raised himself up, until he was erect; and as my uncle moved closer, the two men stared directly at one another, Tom Virgoe moving aside some vaporous visor to do so. And then I witnessed a ghastly sight, which I shall remember to my dying day, and perhaps after it; for Emile's agonized, pleading face began to *melt away* off the bones beneath, his arms and legs and the trunk also melted, like sealing wax under which a flame is held, and at last he collapsed in a heap on the ground, as the shapes of Rose Nightingale and Tom Virgoe drifted and vanished from view behind the great witch elm.

I ran screaming at the utmost pitch of my lungs toward the house, but before I reached it there came a vaporous flash, as when gasoline ignites, and a soft roar, similar to, but infinitely greater than, the sound when a match is set to a gas oven. Two seconds later a violent wave of air hit me such a blow that I lost consciousness.

When I came to, I found that I was lying on the pavement clutching one of my paper racehorses. A policeman was stooping over me, half angry, half solicitous.

"Lucky to be alive, *you* are!" he scolded me. "Running out in the road after a scrap of paper. Should be ashamed of yourself. What about the poor beggar that hit you? How d'you think *he* must have felt? I saw you chasing out like a cat with a tin tied to its tail! All right, are you? Nothing broke? The chap didn't stop—you scared him to his socks, I reckon. You'd better run off home, before I tell your dad to give you a good talking-to."

Bemused, I staggered home. Mrs. Emerald greeted me in a turmoil of worry.

"There you are! But where's your uncle? I was sure you'd gone to meet him. I hope to goodness he's not come to harm in this storm."

For the oppressive heat had culminated in a cataclysmic storm: thunder was exploding overhead, lightning carved the sky into fragments, and rain mixed with hail clattered down with such violence that its sound almost drowned that of the thunder. In two hours that night the river Thames rose fourteen feet, overflowing its banks and flooding the low-lying regions of Hammersmith, Putney, and Fulham. Basements were inundated, underground car parks ruined, and the Brook Green caves were filled with water. It took two weeks to pump them out, and during that time my uncle did not return home, nor was he seen anywhere. There were police appeals, on radio, television, and in the press, but no one came forward; it was thought he might have been kidnapped.

How could I tell anybody what I had seen? Not even to Mrs. Emerald did I dare disclose it; nor to my father when, after four days, he arrived in England. I thought I must be going mad; or that I had dreamed that terrible scene.

But when the Brook Green caves were pumped out, three skeletons were discovered; those of Rose Nightingale and Tom Virgoe, in lead coffins, long dead, resting where they had been buried years ago; and a more recent one, which, from its wristwatch, scapular, and diamond pin, was identified as that of my uncle. But the watch and diamond were melted and calcined in a strange way, as if they had been subjected to radiation, and the bones were blackened, as if by intense heat.

After the funeral, my father took me back to France, leaving a manager in charge of the London office.

Before we left, I did muster my courage to tell Mrs. Emerald what I thought I had seen on the night of the storm, and she wept her heart out.

"Ah, the poor master! He'd have laid down his life for Rose. But it was Tom she loved—always—his songs and his bits of poems. And I daresay the danger bewitched her; girls are like that. Your uncle was very good to Tom. He had his songs sent to a publisher—hoping to please Rose—but she hardly gave him a thought. It was always Tom—from the first moment she saw him. 'Can't I see where you live?' she used to beg. 'I don't mind the dark.' It's dangerous, we warned her, but she would go. Ah, why is life so unjust? But I hope the master is happy now. How can we tell?"

Poor Mrs. Emerald—so kind, so self-effacing. I never saw her again. And when I revisited Brook Green, some years later, I found that the big witch-elm was no longer there on the south side of the Green. Nor was there any sign that it had ever existed; an unbroken line of normal-sized trees, at equal intervals, extend all along from one end to the other.

Strange! For I have met other people who remember that tree . . .

Homer's Whistle

~~~~~~

I had always known Homer Peasmarsh. We were together and friendly all through primary school. He was the small silent boy with straight-cut fringe of fair, almost cotton-white hair, and round intent gray-blue eyes who arrived in a brand-new school uniform somewhat too big for him, clutching a tortoise. Nobody else had a tortoise, so that put up his stock at once. His grandmother had given it to him. She gave him amazing presents with which he came back at the beginning of every term. And, during the term also, bulging, untidily wrapped parcels would arrive from her, and inside them would be crumbling delicious homemade cakes, or books, marbles, a dagger, some coins—not many of these things, but each of them rare and special. Once she sent him a watch strap made from elephants' hairs; once, two enormous butterflies in glass cases. Once, a telescope.

During the holidays he generally went to stay with his grandmother because his parents traveled a great deal. And even when his parents were at home it seemed they did not get on together; they lived in separate places and could not agree which one Homer should stay with first.

In fact, they disliked each other so much that they could not even bear to meet when Homer had to be transferred from his father to his mother, so often he would be left standing on the pavement for an hour or so, waiting for the other parent to turn up.

In those days I liked Homer very much. Partly, of course, because of the interesting things his grandmother sent. Partly because, in the summer, I was sometimes invited to stay at her cottage in Devon, which was just below the edge of the moor, between a rocky brook and a deep, clear river the color of milkless tea. Besides these things, I liked Homer because his mind was deep and clear. He never made pretenses. Never told lies. His thoughts came out, plain and simple. If he had nothing to say, he kept silent.

So we were friends through the years at our small private prep school, which was called Hollyhaw. And when Homer's grandmother discovered that I had been scheduled to go to Watchetts, she persuaded his father to send Homer there too. "His friend Andrew is a decent sort of boy," I suppose she said. "Homer doesn't have much family life; it would be better if he went on through schooldays with his friend."

Around that time Homer's parents finally got divorced; one of them went to live in Brazil, the other in the south of France. So you could say that he had no family life at all. Also, not long after that, Homer's grandmother died. I think she had known that she was going to die for about a year beforehand. And shortly before her death, the small valley below the moor had a dam thrown across its lower end, was filled up with water from the river and turned into a reservoir. Homer's grandmother's cottage was the only home affected. It now lies thirty feet underwater, with weeds growing on its chimneys and fish swimming through its broken windows. I rather hate to think of it.

Drowning the cottage did upset Homer very badly. He had always been a little afraid of deep water. He used to like playing in the brook and splashing in the shallower parts of the river. But he took care to avoid the deep stretches. Sometimes, after a heavy rain up on the moor, the river did a thing we called "coming down"; a great bolster of brown water would roll swiftly along, gathering size and speed on its way, and crash over our little stone bridge. I loved to watch this, it was thrilling, but it made Homer slightly nervous, he worried about the likelihood of sheep and rabbits getting drowned; he much preferred the brook and river at their placid, chuckling summertime levels.

After his grandmother's death and the submerging of her cottage, he began having bad nightmares and would wake screaming from some awful muddled vision of wicked broken brown water and foam and crumbling masonry.

Then we shifted from our small comfortable private prep school to the big, careless, rather tough public-school world of Watchetts, where, instead of being at the top of the school and greatly respected, we were just small fry, swimming for our lives among five hundred others.

What counted at Watchetts was whether you were good at sports. I enjoyed boxing and running and soccer, so I managed well enough and was accepted; but Homer had never been interested in games; his large blue-gray eyes were shortsighted and needed steel-framed glasses; he could not catch a ball and was always afraid that his glasses would get broken (with some reason, for they often did). So he was universally despised.

And he became almost completely silent, only uttering when a master asked him a question in class, and not always then.

"Wake up, Peasmarsh!" they would bark. "You're in a dream, as usual!" and sometimes Homer would respond, and sometimes he would seem too far off in his own remoteness for any human voice to fetch him back.

Since his grandmother died he had spent school holidays with a distantly connected uncle and aunt who lived in West Kensington; they were very boring, he said, and so was their house, but they did leave him to his own devices most of the time, and he seemed to pass days and weeks on end in museums. I think he was very unhappy, both during the term and at holiday time, but the school terms were certainly worse, because the other boys used to bully him and call him "Drip-drop" and the masters shouted at him.

I suppose I should have invited him to stay during the holidays, but I never did. Having him to stay in Colchester wouldn't be a bit the same as those idyllic visits at the cottage by the moor.

Homer was never much good at schoolwork because so much of the time his attention seemed to be elsewhere.

"Why don't you ever pay attention in class?" I asked him once. "What in the world are you thinking about when you go off into one of those dreams of yours?"

"Eh? What? Oh, the cottage, of course. Downcombe," he answered vaguely. "Wishing I could get back there. Remember the Wuzzy, where we made such a lot of tunnels under the brambles? And the haybarn, where we did acrobatics when it rained? And the summer we constructed dozens of artificial islands in the river and planted them with wild flowers? And the calves that we

played bullfights with, in the meadow? And the mushrooms we used to bring in, that grandmother fried for
supper? And the nuts in Tankerton Wood? I just wish I
could go back there. . . ."

"But you can't go back there now," I pointed out. "It's
all underwater. The whole place, Tankerton Wood and
all."

"I know that," he answered rather crossly.

"Well, then, it seems to me it's pointless to think about
it."

He muttered, "If only it were possible to get back
there in the time before it was made into a lake. It had
been there for hundreds of years. And after all, time is
only something *we* invented, for our own convenience.
Like the Fahrenheit scale. Heat and cold and time were
there before we began measuring them. If only we could
step outside the scale, outside of measured time, I bet it
would be possible to go forward or back to any part we
wanted to visit. I wouldn't want to go forward; I just want
to go back."

"That's an idiotic way to talk. How could you possibly?"

I didn't mean to get angry with him, but it did make me
mad to see him wasting his time so. He wasn't learning
anything; he wasn't making friends; he wasn't making
progress of any kind. When he could get away from
people—which wasn't very often—he'd just sit in a corner, absolutely still, completely silent; he hardly seemed
to be breathing. Just once in a while you'd see his nostrils
flicker just a little, like the throat of a frog.

"Breathing control and concentration are very important. That's what would do it," he once absently remarked to me when we happened to sit side by side at
school lunch. (We weren't seeing so much of each other

now.) It was a treacle tart day, and everyone else was bolting their helping, in hope of seconds, while Homer let his piece go cold on its plate and seemed to be staring at something about a hundred miles beyond the school dining-room window.

"Wake up, Drip-drop, Tideswell's pinched your pud!" somebody yelled, and Homer came slowly back from wherever he had been and muttered, "Pudding? Pudding? Oh, what does it matter, what's the difference?"

After a while I made another friend. I had found that it really didn't do to be seen about all the time with nobody but Homer. People began to think that I must be a bit retarded too, in spite of my playing in the lower school second soccer team. So, after a few months, I began going around with a boy called Sparky Timms, who was pretty good at all games and could do funny imitations of TV personalities as well. At first Homer used to trail around after us rather forlornly, about four yards in the rear.

"What in the world do you see in that oaf?" he asked once, when Sparky was somewhere else and we happened to be alone together.

"He's funny. Why? Are you jealous?"

"*Jealous?* Good heavens, no. I just find him terribly boring."

"Well, I'm sorry," I said coldly, "but *I* happen to like him."

Of course now that Homer's grandmother was dead he no longer received those parcels of delicious cakes, obscure books with weird pictures, luminous Victorian glass marbles, pocket astrolabes, and Japanese Shinto objects; in fact, his possessions were now very dismal, because although the aunt and uncle in London doubtless meant well, his parents were so far out of reach that they were always behind with the money for his clothes and stuff he needed for school. So he looked shabby and uncared-for; his hair generally needed cutting and his sleeves were far too short and his toes poked through the canvas of his gym shoes. By now the gifts his grandmother had sent him at Hollyhaw were mostly lost or broken or given away (for he had always been generous with his things—I had been given quite a few of them); all that remained was a little old whistle, made of copper. It had a ring around it, halfway along, which you could twist, to make its tone shriller and shriller, until it finally reached the point where a human ear could not reach its note. Dogs and bats were still able to hear it then, Homer said, but I could never see the point of that. Who wants to whistle to a bat? It had belonged to a seventeenth-century astrologer and mathematician, Homer said, an Exeter-born man called Prester Holinshed, who had written several books on the science of numbers and related subjects. P. Holinshed believed that when numbers reached a certain point of magnitude they changed to something else, as ice changes to water and then to steam at certain temperatures.

"Change to what?" I asked once, but Homer said Holinshed did not seem to have carried his researches far enough to come to any conclusion about what the next step was after numbers. Holinshed had built the cottage, Downcombe, where old Mrs. Peasmarsh lived, and his whistle had been discovered in a little niche to the side of the mantelpiece beam; his initials, P.H., were carved on the whistle, and the date, 1685. Homer loved the whistle because the initials were his own, in reverse, and the date was nearly three hundred years back.

At the beginning of one autumn term Sparky Timms

came back with a whole new batch of information about sex, which he was in the middle of passing on to me when Homer appeared, looking paler, shabbier, odder, and more disconsolate than ever.

"I've got something to tell you," he muttered to me.

"Oh, do buzz off, Homer, can't you see I'm talking to Sparky just now," I said, and, after a minute or two of awkward hanging about in case I changed my mind, he left us again with the kind of clumsy shambling lope that he had developed as he grew larger.

"Why in the world don't you tell that dummy to go and jump in the river?" said Sparky, and went on with what he was telling me.

Slowly, after that, a change began to be observable in Homer. Very probably nobody noticed it but me. I was the only person who troubled to take notice of him.

These days, even more of the time, he seemed to be lost in a total dream; but, oddly enough, even while he was in the dream, he seemed better able to function with the very small part of himself that he left behind to connect into the mesh of school life.

"Decline *jusjurandum*, Peasmarsh," Mr. Fox, the Latin master, would say wearily, and Homer, like a zombie, never coming out of his abstraction, would mechanically recite the correct words.

"Give it a bit more *brio*, Peasmarsh," Mr. Rendall, the English master, would snap, as Homer read aloud a dozen lines from *Twelfth Night,* and Homer would obediently put a bit more expression in and raise his voice. It was as if he were able to switch on the auto pilot.

On the whole, the masters left him alone; he gave the right answers in class, his homework was just adequate; they had more things to do than worry about a boy who seemed to be in a daze the whole time.

At games and sports, oddly enough, he even improved, just a little; his hand, raised in the air, would sometimes connect, as if accidentally, with the ball; he made a run, from time to time, in cricket; it really seemed that the less attention he paid to what he was doing, the more chance there was of his doing it successfully. He still had no friends and talked to nobody; all his spare time was spent in a corner of the library windowseat or, in summer, sitting under one of the big lime trees by the side of the sports ground. A river ran just beyond them that bounded the school property; I wondered if it reminded him of the river at Downcombe. This was a different kind of river, though, deep and reedy and silent.

For a number of months, Homer and I exchanged hardly a word. Then, on my birthday (which comes in May), I found a little package in my locker. It was clumsily wrapped; the bulkiness of it reminded me, for some reason, of those parcels that Homer used to receive from his grandmother. I undid it with foreboding. And inside I discovered the little old copper whistle; I recognized it at once, and if I hadn't, the initials would have reminded me.

Homer was nowhere about, but later I ran into him lurking in the cloakroom where we changed for sports. All the others had gone in to tea.

"Andrew," he said.

It was quite a shock to hear my first name. Of course we all used surnames at Watchetts.

"Well, what?"

"Did you get the whistle?"

"Yes, I did. Thanks."

I felt awkward about it. I didn't want the whistle at all. What use was it to me? Besides, I felt that Homer was trying to buy his way back into my friendship, and I didn't want that either. Sparky and I were now friendly with another boy called Pango Swift, who played drums and guitar and was in the first soccer team; and we were practicing hard for the midsummer sports—in short, I had no time for Homer.

"It really isn't much use to me, Homer—er, Peasmarsh," I said. "Wouldn't you rather hang on to it? After all—" After all, I was going on to say, it's the only thing you've got left from the old days—but I suddenly remembered Homer's grandmother, with her shrewd tongue and her bright-blue eyes, the brick floor of the cottage, the faded cotton chair covers, the grandfather clock, the taste of mushrooms and sausages and toasted homemade bread for supper; my voice for some reason died on me.

"No, I don't want it back," said Homer seriously. "I want you to do something for me."

Oh, oh. "Well, what?" I said again, very reluctantly.

"You see, I'm nearly able to get back there now."

"Get back? Get back *where?*"

The bell was ringing for tea, and it was raspberry-jam day; I could not feel much patience with Homer and his slow, hesitant way of speaking. He was so dusty and shabby and fumbling; yet, in a way, with the straight pale hair, and his intent gray eyes, and earnest manner, he seemed exactly the same as he had at seven.

"To Downcombe, of course," he said. "As I thought, it's all a technique of breathing control. You have to get out of synch. And then you can cross over to wherever you want. But what I'm not sure is, *how long can you stay?* Are you fixed at one point—or does time start to carry you forward again?"

"Have you gone absolutely bananas?" I said.

"Oh, do pay attention, Andrew. I've been reading an

Indian scientist and philosopher called Swami Mansar Ray—a lot of what he says is just what old Holinshed believed. Only it's differently put, of course. Breathing control takes you out—like getting out of gear—and then, if you want to reconnect, a certain kind of sound will jolt you back to the time stratum you started from. Look, I'll show you; have you got the whistle?"

It was in my pocket. I produced it.

"Right; now, give me about three minutes and I'll show you."

"How do you mean, give you three minutes? Don't forget the tea bell's gone."

"Three minutes before you blow the whistle, of course. Twist it right around. Then time me on your watch."

I could see his breathing become slower and slower. Presently it seemed to stop entirely.

"Homer, are you all right? Homer! Answer me!"

"The volume of a given mass of gas varies inversely with the pressure, provided the temperature remains constant," he replied in a calm, mechanical voice. "Thank you, Wilson, I am perfectly all right."

I wasn't at all certain of this; also, I wanted my tea; so after two minutes, not three, I blew the soundless whistle and was relieved to see a touch of red come back into Homer's wax-colored cheeks and his breathing begin to deepen.

Then for the first time I noticed that in his hand he was holding a particolored knitted potholder.

"You didn't give me enough time," he said reproachfully. "*Three* minutes was what I told you, not two. I only just had time to grab this."

"Where the dickens did that come from?"

"Don't you recognize it?"

I did, as a matter of fact; his grandmother used to make them and always had a couple hanging on a hook beside the kitchen oil stove.

"Why in the world do you carry that about?"

"I just brought it from *there*."

"I—oh, look here, that's rubbish! I don't believe you. I'm going to tea, see you later."

But just the same I did feel almost shaken; the pot-holder was so very familiar. But still—Well, I didn't want to think about it.

Homer grabbed my arm, though, as I was about to leave him.

"Andrew—listen. You said you'd do something for me."

I had not, but I found it hard to drag myself rudely from his clutch.

"If you see me—well, *gone*, like that, for a really long time—more than an hour, say—will you blow the whistle and get me back? It's marvelous, but I still have a lot to learn—haven't quite got the hang—"

"I can't keep an eye on you all the time," I said crossly. "How am I supposed to do that? Have a bit of sense!"

"Just the same—please do, Andrew?"

"Oh, all right."

I wondered if I ought to say something about him to the matron or his grade master. My promise was pretty useless, really, for we weren't in the same stream now.

Still, once in a while we found ourselves in a class together. One of these was carpentry, at which Homer had been unremarkably bad; he was clumsy with tools and not at all interested; he dropped things, spoiled wood, it took him weeks to learn to make a simple joint. But now, I noticed that in a state of dreamy calm he was completing a very neat mortice with slots in a table leg and corresponding tongues of wood on the two side pieces. All his attention was elsewhere, far away; perhaps at Downcombe. Sliding the whistle out of my pocket, I surreptitiously turned facing the wall and blew a sound-less blast.

Homer jerked, and cut his finger with the chisel, and said something sharp under his breath. Five minutes later, passing my bench, he whispered reproachfully, "Why did you have to blow it just *then*? I hadn't been gone long! It was a wonderful hot blowy July day, and we'd been picking wild strawberries all afternoon and Granny was going to make jam."

"Was I there too?"

"Of course. And much nicer then. I wish you hadn't blown—"

"Well, you asked me," I said crossly.

"I know I did." He had the grace to look apologetic. "Thanks, anyway. I daresay it's a good thing to come back and check up."

The next time I blew for Homer was after a church service one Sunday. I'd noticed him utterly rapt in a corner of a pew. That time he gave me a somewhat star-tled nod and blink, and muttered to me after a moment, "I'd been there for about six weeks. . . ."

"What was that poor dumb jerk talking to you about?" inquired Sparky, strolling up behind us and thumping my head with a prayer book as Homer shambled out of the chapel.

"Oh," I said reluctantly, "just a kind of nutty idea that he has."

"What about?"

"Going back into the past." We were walking back toward the main school buildings. I hoped Sparky would abandon the subject.

"Going back into the past? But how *sublime,*" said Sparky. Sublime was his word just then.

It was a fine hot morning and we were going to do some sports training. "Tell me more," Sparky said as we changed into running shoes. "How does our Peasmarsh set about it?"

"By—by a kind of breathing control. And then—then, the theory is that a particular kind of sound jerks him back into the present time again."

"Why, this is quite riveting," said Sparky as we strolled out toward the sports ground. "Do, please, continue. *What* particular kind of sound?"

Feeling that I shouldn't, I fished out the whistle from the pocket of my running shorts. "When I blow this."

Sparky studied the small copper tube attentively and asked its history; I told him what I knew about it.

"Are you ready?" bawled Enthoven, the sports master. "First group for the hundred yards sprint: on your marks, get set—GO!"

We were in the second group, so Sparky continued to study the whistle.

"You say," he pondered, "that our dear friend Peasmarsh is *happy* in the past; happier than he is at this delightful educational establishment?"

"Well—yes—I suppose that's where he really—"

"Second group!" yelled Enthoven. I hurriedly grabbed the whistle back from Sparky; we crouched, got set, then ran as if the devil were at our heels. Sparky beat me by a tenth of a second.

"Then," he went on as if nothing had happened; his breathing control was almost as good as Homer's, "would it not be better for all concerned if our mutual friend were to *stay* in the past? Let's see that whistle again."

Slowly I handed it to him. We were now at the far end of the sports ground, under the lime trees. Sparky calmly tossed the whistle so that it flew in a wide, glittering arc and landed in the river, where it made no more splash than a minnow rising.

"Third group!" bawled Mr. Enthoven. "On your marks, get set—"

Homer was in the third group. Normally he was an undistinguished runner, generally arriving last, well after all others; but on this occasion he amazed everybody by drawing effortlessly to the front of the group, then far, far ahead; his speed must have been about double that of anybody else who ran that afternoon.

"WELL DONE, Peasmarsh!" yelled the sports master.

But Homer did not stop running when he passed the tape; he kept right on, faster and faster, straight into the river, and disappeared from view.

Nor did he come up again; the Yarrow runs very fast. When his body was at last discovered, it had been washed about a mile downstream.

I worry about Homer a great deal. I wake in the night, sweating and trembling; I imagine him, alone in that cottage, with no gas, no electricity, only candles; with Rusty, the old spaniel who died when we were eight. Sometimes I think I can hear Rusty howl; sometimes I think I can hear the brown wall of water rolling down the valley, smashing banks, knocking trees aside, hoisting up rocks, pouring over the meadows, coming to overwhelm the little house.

The Last Specimen

The Reverend Matthew Pentecost, aged seventy, had a regular monthly habit. On his way to conduct Evensong in the tiny church of St.-Anthony-under-the-Downs, he invariably parked his aged Rover for ten minutes by the side of a small patch of woodland about ten minutes' drive from the church.

Services at St. Anthony's took place only once a month; for the rest of the time the isolated building with its Saxon stonework, Douai font, willful hand organ, and two massive yew trees, drowsed undisturbed, save by casual tourists who occasionally wandered in, looked around, dropped a ten-pence piece into the box that begged help for the fabric of the roof, and inspected the small overgrown churchyard with its nineteen graves.

At the monthly services the congregation seldom exceeded half a dozen, and in wet weather or snow Mr. Pentecost and Miss Sedom, who played the organ, had the place to themselves. St. Anthony's lay three quarters of a mile from any house; the mild slopes of the Berkshire downs enfolded it as sometimes after a falling tide a cup of sand will hold a single pebble.

One of the rector's favorite views was that of the church's swaybacked stone roof, bracketed between its two majestic dark yew trees, with the leisurely gray-green of the hillsides beyond. This was one reason for his pre-Evensong period of meditation beside the little wood. The second reason was the tactful desire to allow his parishioners time to assemble, sit down, and rest from their cross-country walk for a few minutes before he appeared among them. Except for the trees on his left, the countryside thereabouts lay bare as an open hand, so that the members of the congregation could be seen from a great distance, making their way along the foot-path that led to the church from Compton Druce, the nearest hamlet.

On this evening in mid-April Mr. Pentecost sat in his rusty Rover with an especially happy and benign expression on his face. After a rainy afternoon the sky had cleared: thrushes, larks, and blackbirds were singing in fervent appreciation of the sun's last rays, which turned the greenish-white pearls of the budding hawthorn to a silvery dazzle. In this light the down grass and young wheat shone with an almost luminous intensity of color.

"Interesting," mused Mr. Pentecost, "how these early greens of the year, dog's mercury and elder leaves, and the green of bluebells, contain such a strong mixture of blue in their color."

Mr. Pentecost's hobby was painting delicate water-color landscapes, and he was minutely observant of such niceties.

"Then, later in the spring, in May and June, the brighter, more yellowy greens appear: young beech and oak leaves with their buttery rich color; doubtless the extra degree of light from the sun has something to do with it."

Mr. Pentecost watched fondly as Ben Tracey, the farmer who owned the enormous pasture on his right, arrived in a Land-Rover with sacks of feed for the sheep. The spring had been an unusually cold one, and the grass remained unseasonably scanty. Sighting Ben, the sheep and lambs, well acquainted with the object of his daily visit, began purposefully making toward him from all corners of the vast field, lambs following their mothers like iron filings drawn to a magnet in regular converging lines, only broken at one point by the presence of a massive oak tree covered with reddish buds that grew toward the middle of the field. Mr. Pentecost eyed the tree thoughtfully. Was it not unusually advanced in its growth for such a cold season? And why had he not noticed it last month?

Farmer and rector waved to one another, then Mr. Pentecost, observing the last of his congregation pass through the churchyard and enter St. Anthony's porch, was about to start his motor again, when, in the rearview mirror, he noticed a girl, who had been slowly riding her pony along the road behind the car. At this moment she dismounted, tethered the pony to a tree, and vanished through a gate into the little wood.

Normally such a sight would have aroused no particular curiosity in Mr. Pentecost, but two unusual factors here caught his attention. First, neither girl nor mount were familiar to him; yet Mr. Pentecost was certain that he knew every girl and every pony within a ten-mile radius. So where had she come from? Second, the girl carried a trowel and a basket.

Without apparent haste, yet acting with remarkable calm and dispatch for a man of his age, Mr. Pentecost backed the Rover a hundred yards to the point where the pony stood tethered to a young ash tree. The rector got out of his car, studied the pony thoughtfully for a moment, then walked into the wood. The gate stood open: another factor worthy of note. Slightly compressing his lips, Mr. Pentecost closed it behind him and took the path that bisected the wood. The girl ahead of him was easily visible because of her bright-blue anorak; she was, in any case, walking slowly, glancing from side to side as if in search of something.

Mr. Pentecost could easily guess at the object of her quest. He caught up with her just as she had reached it: a patch of delicate spindly plants, each of them nine inches to a foot high, growing in a small sunny clearing. They had bell-shaped flowers the size of small, upside-down tulips—odd, elegant, mysterious flowers, white, with a pinkish-purple tracery over the fluted petals.

The girl knelt beside them and took her trowel from the basket.

"No, no. You mustn't," said Mr. Pentecost gently behind her. The girl gasped and spun around, gazing up at him with wide, frightened eyes.

"My dear child, believe me, you *mustn't,*" repeated the rector, the seriousness of his tone mitigated to some degree by the mild expression in his blue eyes. The girl gazed at him, nonplussed, embarrassed, temporarily speechless, it seemed.

She was, he noticed, a very pretty girl, about seventeen, perhaps, in the accustomed uniform of jeans and T-shirt and riding boots. On her head, though, she sported a slightly absurd and certainly unusual article of headgear—not a crash helmet, but a strapped furry hat with a cylindrical top, like the shakoes worn by cavalry in the Crimean War. Could she have inherited it from some great-great-grandfather? Or perhaps, thought the vicar indulgently, it was a prop borrowed from some local theatrical venture; the young loved to dress up in fancy dress. But, now that he saw her close to, he was certain that he did not know this girl; she was a total stranger. Her eyes were a clear beautiful greenish gold—like the color of the young oak leaves he had been thinking about a few minutes earlier. Her hair, what could be seen of it under the shako, was the same color, with a decided greenish tint; punk, no doubt, thought Mr. Pentecost knowledgeably. The children nowadays dyed their hair extraordinary colors; green was nothing out of the common. He had seen pink, orange, and lilac.

The girl continued to gaze at him in silence, abashed and nervous, grasping her trowel.

"Wild fritillaries are so rare, so very rare," Mr. Pentecost mildly explained to her, "that it is wrong, it is most dreadfully wrong to dig them up; besides, of course, being against the law. Did you not know that? And why, do you suppose, are they so rare?" he went on, considerately giving her time to recover her composure. "Why, because of people like yourself, my dear, finding out about where they grow and coming to dig up specimens. I know the temptation—believe me, I know it!—but you really must *not,* you know."

"Oh, dear," murmured the girl, finding her voice at last, it seemed. "I'm—I'm very sorry. I—I didn't know."

"No? You really didn't know? Where are you from?" he inquired, gently veiling his disbelief. "You are certainly not from anywhere around here, or I should have known you. And your steed," he added thoughtfully.

"No, I—I come from—from quite a long way away. I was sent"—she hesitated, looking sheepish and contrite —"sent to—to collect a specimen, as you say. It is the last, you see—we already have one of everything else."

Good gracious, thought Mr. Pentecost, in surprise and

a certain amount of disapproval. *Everything* else? Aloud he said,

"It is for a school project, I conclude? Well, I am sorry to disappoint you, but you really must *not* remove the flowers from this precious patch. I will tell you what you can do, though—" as her face fell. "If you care to accompany me to Evensong in St. Anthony's—or, of course, wait outside the church if you prefer," he added kindly, "you may then come with me to my rectory in Chilton Parsley. I am fortunate enough to have quite a large number of fritillaries growing in my flower border, and I shall be happy to give you a specimen for your collection. How about that, my dear?"

"Why," said the girl slowly, "that—that is very kind of Your Reverence. I am indeed greatly obliged to you." She spoke with considerable formality; although English enough in appearance, she could, judging from her accent, have been a foreigner who had learned the language very correctly from some aristocratic old lady with nineteenth-century intonations. "I have instructions to be back though"—she glanced at the sky, then at the watch on her wrist—"by seven. Will that—?"

"Plenty of time," he assured her, smiling. "The evening service is never a long one. . . . Strict about that sort of thing, are they, at your school?"

She blushed.

Mr. Pentecost began walking back toward the gate, anxious, without making it too obvious that he was in a hurry, to join his patient parishioners, but also wishful to be certain that the girl accompanied him. She, however, showed no sign of intending to disobey his prohibition and came with him docilely enough. Once outside the copse gate—"You must *always* close gates, you know," Mr. Pentecost reminded her amiably but firmly—she remounted, and he got into his car. "Just follow behind," he told her, poking his white-haired head out of the window. She nodded, kicking the shaggy pony into a walk; perhaps it was the late light filtered through the young hawthorns, but the pony, too, Mr. Pentecost thought, showed a decided touch of green in its rough coat. "Only a very short way to the church," he called, swerving his car erratically across the road as he put his head out again to impart this information.

The girl nodded and kicked her pony again. For its diminutive size—a Shetland cross, perhaps?—the pony certainly showed a remarkable turn of speed.

Mr. Pentecost had not expected that the girl would be prepared to attend his service, but she quietly tied her pony to the lych-gate, murmured some exhortation into its ear, and followed him through the churchyard, glancing about her with interest. Then a doubt seemed to overtake her: "Am I dressed suitably to come inside?" she asked in a low, worried tone, pausing at the church door.

"Perfectly," he assured her, smiling at the glossy shako. "Our congregation at St. Anthony is quite informal."

So she slipped in after him and demurely took her place in a pew at the back.

After the service—which, as he had promised, lasted no longer than twenty-five minutes—the rector exchanged a few friendly words with the six members of his congregation, stood waving good-bye to them as they set off on their return walk across the fields, and then said to the girl, who had remounted and was waiting by the gate:

"Now, if you will follow me again, my dear, I will drive slowly and I do not think the journey should take more than about fifteen minutes for that excellent little animal of yours."

She nodded, and they proceeded as before, the vicar driving at twenty miles an hour, not much less than his normal speed, while horse and rider followed with apparent ease.

As he drove, Mr. Pentecost reflected. During Evensong his mind, as always, had been entirely given over to the service, but he had, with some part of it, heard the girl's voice now and then, particularly in the hymn, Miss Sedom's favorite, "Glory to Thee My God This Night." So the girl was, at least, familiar with Christian ritual. Or was a remarkably speedy learner. Or was it conceivable that she could be coached, as it were, continuously by— by whatever agency had sent her? There were so many things wrong with her—and yet, mused the rector, he could swear that there was no harm about her, not an atom.

When they reached the damp and crumbling laurel-girt rectory, Mr. Pentecost drove around, as was his habit, to the mossy yard at the rear, and parked there.

"You can tie your pony to the mounting block—" He gestured to the old stable. "Now, I will just leave my cassock inside the back door—so—and fetch a trowel— ah, no, of course there is no need for that, you already have one." It was a bricklayer's trowel, but no matter. "Follow me, then."

The rectory garden, beyond the overgrown laurel hedge, was a wonderful wilderness of old-fashioned flowers and shrubs that had grown, proliferated, and battled for mastery during the last hundred years. Smaller and more delicate plants had, on the whole, fared badly; but Mr. Pentecost adored his fritillaries and had cherished them as carefully as he was able: frail and beautiful, both speckled and white, they drooped their magic bells among a drift of pale blue anemones and a fringe of darker blue grape hyacinths.

"Aren't they extraordinary?" he said, fondly looking down at them. "It is so easy to believe in a benevolent Creator when one considers these and the anemones— which, I believe, are the lilies of the field referred to in St. Matthew. Now, this little clump, still in bud, would, I think, transfer without too much harm, my dear—er— what did you say your name was?"

She hesitated. Then: "My name is Anjla," she answered, with a slight, uneasy tremor of her voice. And she knelt to dig up the clump of plants he had indicated. The rector fetched her a grimy plastic bag from the toolshed, but she shook her head.

"Thank you, but I can't take it. Only the flowers. This is—this is truly very kind of you."

A faint warning hum sounded in the air—like that of a clock before it strikes.

The vicar glanced across the wide meadow that lay alongside his garden. A large oak, leafless still, covered with reddish buds, grew in the middle of the grassy space. Mr. Pentecost eyed it thoughtfully. Beyond it, pale and clear, shone the evening star.

Mr. Pentecost said, "My dear—where do you really come from?"

The girl stood, tucking the plants into her basket. She followed the direction of his glance, but said defensively, "You would not know the name of the place."

It was, however, remarkably hard to evade Mr. Pentecost when he became as serious as he was now.

"Forgive my curiosity," he said, "but I do think it important that I should know—precisely why are you collecting specimens?"

She was silent for a moment; for too long. Mr. Pentecost went on, "You see—I am an absentminded, vague old man, but even *I* could not help noticing that your pony has claws on its hoofs. *Moropus!* A prehistoric horse not seen in these parts for thirty million years! And, well, there were various other things—"

She blushed furiously.

"That was the trouble!" she burst out. "For such a small errand—just one flower—they wouldn't allocate enough research staff. I *knew* there were details they had skimped on—"

"But why," he persisted mildly, "why are you collecting?"

Anjla looked at him sorrowfully. Then she said, "Well —as you seem to have spotted us, and it is so very late, in any case, I suppose it won't matter now if I tell you—"

"Yes, my dear?"

"This planet"—she glanced round at the stable yard— "is due to blow up—oh, very, very soon. Our scientists have calculated it to within the next three chronims—"

"Chronims?"

"Under one hundred of your hours, I think. Naturally, therefore, we were checking the contents of our own Terrestrial Museum—"

"Ah, I see." He stood thinking for a few minutes, then inquired with the liveliest interest, "And you really do have one of everything? Even—for instance—a rector of the Church of England?"

"I'm afraid so." Her tone was full of regret. "I *wish* I could take you with me. You have been so kind. But we have a vicar, a dean, a bishop, a canon—we have them all. Even an archbishop."

"My dear child! You mistook my meaning. I would not,

not for one moment, consider leaving. My question was prompted by—by a simple wish to know."

The low hum was audible again. Anjla glanced at the sky.

"I'm afraid that now I really have to go."

"Of course you must, my dear. Of course."

They crossed the yard and found the shaggy Moropus demolishing, with apparent relish, the last of a bunch of carrots that had been laid on the mounting block for Mr. Pentecost's supper.

Anjla checked and stared, aghast. "*Sphim!* What have you *done?*"

She burst into a torrent of expostulation, couched in a language wholly unlike any earthly tongue; it appeared to have no consonants at all, to consist of pure sound, like the breathy note of an ocarina.

The Moropus guiltily hung its head and shuffled its long-clawed feet.

Mr. Pentecost stood looking at the pair in sympathy and perplexity.

The warning hum sounded in the air again.

"Do I understand that your—um—companion has invalidated his chance of departure by the consumption of those carrots?"

"I don't know what *can* have come over him—we were briefed so carefully—told to touch nothing, to take in nothing except—over and over again they told us—"

"Perhaps it was a touch of Method," suggested Mr. Pentecost. "He was really getting into the skin of his part." And he added something about Dis and Persephone that the girl received with the blankness of noncomprehension. She had placed her hands on either side of the pony's hairy cheekbones; she bent forward until her forehead touched the other's. Thus she stood for a couple of moments in silence. Then she straightened and walked across the yard in the direction of the meadow. Her eyes swam with tears. Following her, interested and touched, Mr. Pentecost murmured,

"I will, of course, be glad to take care of your friend. During what little time remains."

"I am sure that you will. Thank you. I—I am glad to have met you."

"You could not—I suppose—show me what you both really look like?" he asked with a touch of wistfulness.

"I'm afraid that would be quite impossible. Your eyes simply aren't adapted, you see—"

He nodded, accepting this. Just the same, for a single instant he did receive an impression of hugeness, brightness, speed. Then the girl vaulted the fence and, carefully carrying her basket, crossed the meadow to the large oak tree in the center.

"Good-bye," called Mr. Pentecost. The Moropus lifted up its head and let out a soft groaning sound.

Beside the oak tree, Anjla turned and raised her hand with a grave, formal gesture. Then she stepped among the low-growing branches of the tree, which immediately folded like an umbrella, and, with a swift flash of no-colored brilliance, shot upward, disintegrating into light.

Mr. Pentecost remained for a few moments, leaning with his forearms on the wooden fence, gazing pensively at the star Hesperus, which, now that the tree was gone, could be seen gleaming in radiance above the horizon.

The rector murmured:

> "Earth's joys grow dim, its glories pass away
> Change and decay in all around I see;
> O Thou, Who changest not, abide with me."

Then, pulling a juicy tussock of grass from beside one of the fence posts, he carried it back to the disconsolate Moropus.

"Here, my poor friend; if we are to wait for Armageddon together, we may as well do so in comfort. Just excuse me a moment while I fetch a deck chair and a steamer rug from the house. And do, pray, finish those carrots. I will be with you again directly."

He stepped inside the back door. The Moropus, with a carrot top and a hank of juicy grass dangling from its hairy lips, gazed after him sadly but trustfully.

About the Author

Joan Aiken's many books for adults and young people have become modern classics. Born into a writing family —her father was the American poet Conrad Aiken—she has been writing since childhood and is celebrated for her inventiveness, wit, and wry sense of humor.

Her most recent book for Delacorte Press was *Bridle the Wind,* a sequel to *Go Saddle the Sea.* She is perhaps best known for her books about Dido Twite, the most recent of which, *The Stolen Lake,* was published by Delacorte Press Books for Young Readers, which has also published her *The Shadow Guests* and *A Touch of Chill: Tales for Sleepless Nights.*

Ms. Aiken lives in England.

20233　　OHS

SC　　Aiken, Joan
AiK
　　　A whisper in the
　　　night

DATE			
MY 05 '86			
SE 2 5 '86			
OC 1 3 '86			
OC 2 2 '86			
MR 03 '87			
UC 09 '87			
Fac			
MR 11 '91			
MR 2 4 '92			
FAC DEC 1 8			
OCT 1 2 1999			

20233